PRAISE FOR THE GUNS OF LEGENDE

Western fans looking to break away from the run of the mill standard Western tropes need look no further, The Guns of Legende will hit you like a shot of whiskey after a dusty trail drive...

— PAUL BISHOP - HOST OF THE SIX-GUN JUSTICE PODCAST

Guns, gold, undercover agents, fights, and narrow escapes will keep you turning pages until you're done and leave you wanting the next installment of the series!

— STAN DAY - FOUR STAR AMAZON REVIEWER

FROZEN!

Emily O'Connor tumbled off the catwalk. For an instant she thought she could take flight like a bird and flutter off. Then gravity wrapped its powerful fingers around her. She plunged downward. At the last instant, she twisted around and landed flat on her back.

The entire length of her spine was chilled by ice. She had landed hard in the vat and flopped about on top of the frozen block. She tried to sit up. The ice under her creaked and groaned, then broke. She dropped only a few inches, but that was enough to take her breath away.

Emily opened her eyes and saw the world above her in frigid blue ripples. Then she tried to breathe. Only ice water entered her nose and mouth. The world began to fade. Fast.

THE GUNS OF LEGENDE

Thunderstick Diplomats: A Short Story
Front Range Rebellion
Death Waits at Yellowstone
Gunsmoke and Ice
Queen of the Bandits
Dirty Deeds

YOUR FREE STORY IS WAITING

Delve into the origins of the Guns of Legende and get your FREE bonus copy of a rip-snorting new Western adventure at www.GunsOfLegende.com:

Thunderstick Diplomats

GUNSMOKE AND ICE

The Guns of Legende #3

BRODY WEATHERFORD

The Society of Buckhorn and Bison, Publishers

Copyright ©2022 The Cenotaph Corporation

ISBN: 9798813781230

No part of this novel or the related files may be reproduced or transmitted in any form, by any means (electronic, photocopying, recording, or otherwise) without the prior written permission of the publisher.

Cover by Dreamstime / Lohman Hills Creative

I

"This robbery's going to be as easy as falling off a log," Dandy Dan Dinkins said, as much to convince himself as the four men with him.

"I don't know, Dinkins," Pete Randall said uneasily. "They got guards inside. I tell you, we shoulda robbed a train. That's easier. Block the tracks in some out of the way place, stop the locomotive, shoot in the air a couple of times and the engineer gives up, then we rifle through the mail car."

"Pete's right," Hugh Wilson piped up. His voice was shrill with fear. "How hard is it getting a mail clerk to give up? Everyone knows they're cowards. That railroad clerk'd give up everything in his safe as quick as a chicken going after a bug. He wouldn't want to get killed. Not like bank guards. They're hired to shoot people."

Dinkins heard defeat in those words. Like the others, Randall and Wilson had never robbed a bank before. In spite of what they bragged on, he doubted they had ever held up a train, either.

He cursed his choice of partners. At least one of the gang other than him needed to be steely-eyed and cold hearted. At least one of them should have done this before or faced someone with a gun drawn on them. As it was, all four were greenhorns he had recruited down south in a Santa Fe cantina.

He'd been a little drunk. Dinkins had to admit that now. There was nothing little about how much the four had been soused. The two that worried him most were the Chandler brothers. They weren't twins but looked enough alike that he couldn't keep them apart. They dressed alike, rode horses that looked the same and finished each other's sentences when they bothered to say anything at all. Worst of all, neither of them had sobered up since that last bottle of tequila in the cantina.

All the way on the ride to Taos Randall and Wilson had boasted about how brave they were and how much money they'd take from the bank. After inflating everyone's share, Wilson had launched into improbable ways to spend it. There weren't enough whores or whiskey west of the Mississippi to satisfy him. The way the other three chimed in, these four would wear out every doxie in New Mexico Territory.

Dinkins had listened to such bravado with some unease. Men who shot off their mouths seldom stood up when the going got tough. If he hadn't needed them, he would have left the bank alone with its vault crammed with gold. Common sense fought with greed. It turned out to be a one-sided fight.

The lure was too great! He had to risk it.

"We'll hit the place just before they close. That way we don't have to worry about customers getting in the way," Dinkins said. He pulled his pocket watch out and thumbed open the scratched silver lid. Five minutes. It was almost four in the afternoon when the bank closed.

"Bankers got it easy," Wilson said too loudly. "They close up early every day when a farmer's got another three hours of work ahead of them. They open after the cows have been milked and chores done. They got it too easy. And they only come to work six days a week." He pulled his red-patterned bandanna up over his bulbous nose.

"They don't deserve to have all that money," Randall said. "It's time for us to get our share. They owe me." He fumbled but got his bandanna hooked over his nose.

Dinkins looked sharply at Pete Randall, wondering what he meant by "they owe me." Randall must have had dealings with the bank he hadn't mentioned before. That made it all the more critical to get the robbery over, in quick and out as fast and clean as possible.

By this time both the Chandler boys had followed suit and covered their faces. They drew their six-shooters. The other two stared hard at the adobe-walled bank, as if seeing through the three-foot thick walls and counting the gold coins stacked in the tellers' cages. Dinkins was more interested in the vault. He had heard back in the Santa Fe cantina a man boasting of how his boss, a big rancher working part of the Peralta land grant, had more than a thousand dollars in the vault waiting to buy prime breeding stock. It was only going to be in the bank for another couple days before getting paid out to the cattle broker.

Dandy Dan Dinkins knotted his blue-and-white bandanna behind his head and drew his own six-gun. It was four o'clock.

"Time to get rich," he said. He dashed from where they'd gathered across the street from the bank. Less than halfway across, the bank president came to the heavy wood door and began closing it. The business day was over.

"Don't let him lock that door!" Dinkins cried. The heavy wood, once barred on the inside, would resist anything short of a stick of dynamite to get it open.

He didn't have to tell the others. They all opened fire. He winced as a slug tore past his ear. The Chandlers were behind him and shooting wildly. Before he had a chance to warn them to be more careful, he smashed into the door.

For an instant he thought the banker had secured it. His shoulder hurt like bones had broken. Then the door swung inward as if exploding out of the way. Dinkins fell past and crashed to the floor. Above him came a new lead storm. He looked up to see the banker clutch his chest. Three different spots turned red. As his heart pumped out its last, the blood spread on the banker's fancy coat.

"You shot him!" Dinkins stared at the banker, sprawled only a foot from him. Almost face to face, he stared into dead eyes. He'd seen dead men in his day. Not many, but some. But he'd never been this close to one freshly dead.

Dinkins grunted as someone used his back as a spring to launch forward. The echoes from too many pistols firing drowned out when a shotgun roared.

Blood showered down on him. Dinkins rolled to the side, came to a halt on his belly. He stared straight at a guard fumbling to reload both tubes in a sawed-off shotgun. A curious paralysis seized him. He had his six-shooter aimed at the guard but wasn't able to squeeze the trigger. As if the guard was dipped in molasses, he moved with painfully slow determination. Dinkins saw him pull two more shells from his coat pocket. They slid into the shotgun chambers. The click as the gun breach closed deafened him.

His eyes locked with the guard's. The man was terrified. Dinkins read that in every line of the old man's face. Old man. He was old enough to be Dinkins' father. Grandfather!

The twin barrels lifted. Dinkins stared down them like he stared into two railroad tunnels. Everything still moved slowly, so slowly.

The guard's lips curled back in a grimace. Shots rang out in the bank lobby and men moaned and cried and screeched in pain.

The man's index finger pulled back on the twin triggers. Dinkins saw the knuckle turn white. All so slow. Too slow.

He was going to die.

His Colt bucked in his grip. Then came the new roar of a discharging shotgun. Dinkins winced as tiny pinpricks poked him in the face. And the world returned to normal around him.

The guard toppled forward. He had fired into the wood floor a couple feet in front of where Dinkins sprawled. The splinters cut his cheeks and forehead. The guard had missed!

He scrambled to his feet and crashed into a low railing separating the lobby from a small space where the bank president had a desk. Just beyond the dead president's desk the vault door stood open. For the first time it hit Dinkins how futile the robbery would have been if the banker had already locked the vault and then died when they barged in. Someone else might know the combination to the massive lock, but finding who wasted time.

The tellers were all down, too.

"Don't kill them unless you have to," he called out.

"Too late, Dan," Randall gasped out. "They all went down fighting. Every last one of them." Randall stood as if stunned by it all. His weathered face had gone pasty white and he waved his six-shooter around, hunting for a new target. There wasn't one. They had wiped out everyone else in the building.

He glanced over his shoulder and saw the carnage in the small bank. Two tellers lay behind the counter, dead. One stared up sightlessly and the other was face down and bleeding into the wood planking.

The banker had perished in the initial attack.

One of the Chandler brothers, cried out.

"Hugh. Hugh!"

"Is Wilson hit bad?" Dinkins looked around from where he stood in the mouth of the vault. He wanted to paw through everything inside but, as leader, he had a responsibility to his partners to get them out of the bank alive.

"Get the gold," one of the Chandler boys said. "He's not hurt so that he'd notice."

"A teller got a clean shot at him," Pete Randall said, pressing close behind him. "I evened the score for poor Hugh."

"Stop talkin' 'bout me like I was dead," Wilson said. He propped himself against the counter, clutching his belly. "Get the money. That'll fix me up real good knowin' we got it. I want to be rich! That'll heal me quicker 'n a hungry coyote goin' after a rabbit."

Dinkins turned to the wounded man, but the Chandler brothers shoved past him, carrying him along in their headlong rush to get into the vault.

The three of them crowded into the small space. The Chandlers rummaged through boxes stacked on wood shelves, throwing the contents everywhere.

"Where's the gold? You said there was a mountain of it here."

Dinkins shook his head. He didn't know. Then he saw a crate in the corner.

"What's in that?"

Both the other robbers pounced on the box. The lid came off with a shriek of nails pulling out of wood.

"By damn, I never seen so much gold. All in coins, too! We don't have to divvy up gold bars." The two men ran their hands through the loose coins in the box.

Dinkins stepped out of the vault. Randall stood by Wilson, supporting him.

"Get the horses," he ordered Randall. "We've got the gold."

"I don't know if I should leave him," Randall said.

"Hugh can empty the tellers' drawers while you fetch the horses. So much gunfire's bound to attract attention."

"But..."

"The horses!" Dinkins shouted. He considered firing his pistol at Randall to get him moving. Somehow he pulled the trigger by accident. The hammer fell on a spent cartridge.

The action lit a fire under Pete Randall. He stepped away from Wilson so fast that the wounded man fell to his knees.

"I'll take care of him. Get the horses!" Dinkins went to Wilson. The man pushed him away.

"I can ride. I'm not letting the gold outta my sight." Wilson craned his neck to look past Dinkins at the Chandler brothers dragging sacks of gold coins across the lobby.

Dinkins wasn't going to argue. Wilson stumbled to the door, stepped over the dead bank president and grabbed onto the pommel of his steeldust. For a moment Dinkins doubted the wounded man would be able to mount. With a loud groan and a heave, Wilson pulled himself up into the saddle. He swayed, then gripped the saddle horn with one hand and pointed down the dusty, winding street.

"The law!"

Both Chandler brothers began firing at the approaching man. He returned fire with the rifle he carried, but they drove him back.

"Clear out with the loot," Dinkins ordered the brothers. "I'll lead the law dogs on a wild goose chase. Let's meet up at the Santa Fe cantina in a week."

The Chandlers had already hightailed it. They had the gold slung in bags over the rumps of their mounts. He had the gut-wrenching feeling he might not see them again, but there was nothing to do about it. To Randall he said, "Look after Wilson. He's in a bad way. And don't let the brothers steal the gold." He worked frantically to reload his six-gun.

Pete Randall didn't answer. Wilson did. "Not gonna give it

up easy. Not after I took a bullet gettin' it. Me and Pete'll watch 'em." He winced and added, "Santa Fe. A week. Don't you go get yourself caught!" He bent low, fired a couple times down the street and put his heels to his horse.

Dinkins faced more than a solitary marshal now. Four more men joined in the fight. Lead whipped past his head, but the men were lousy shots. He vaulted into the saddle. From the added elevation, he got a clear shot at the first man. He took careful aim and fired. The man threw up his arms and reared up. Dinkins had drilled him squarely through the badge pinned on his coat.

This caused panic among the small posse. Dinkins took advantage and galloped past them, shooting left and right until his six-shooter came up empty again. He missed each time but scattered the men. He had bought himself some time.

Him and the other four with the gold.

∼

NOT FOR THE FIRST TIME DANDY DAN DINKINS WONDERED if the posse on his trail refused to give up because he'd killed the Taos marshal. For two solid days and nights they'd come after him. He'd decoyed them away from his four partners, but right now he wanted their guns backing him up. The determination the posse showed meant only one thing.

If they caught him, there wouldn't be a trial. They'd string him up from the nearest cottonwood.

"Got my share of the gold to spend," he told himself. Dinkins had never thought of himself as a charitable man, but it was turning out that way. He risked his neck so the others could escape. "If I get out of this, I'm buying myself the best damned bottle of whiskey I can find, the prettiest señorita in all of New Mexico Territory and we'll hole up in the fanciest hotel this side of New Orleans."

The rataplan of hooves crushing dried pine needles caused him to tug on the reins and try to blend into the forest. If he'd ridden much farther into the Sangre de Cristo Mountains, he'd be above the timberline. Those pine trees, aspen and spruce hid him from the sharp-eyed posse. At least he hoped they did. He was running low on ammunition.

"... not the right trail," complained a distant voice.

"Told you we should have followed the other hoofprints."

Dinkins held his breath. The riders weren't more than twenty yards away. They were hidden from his view. He hoped the opposite was true. He dared not move deeper into the trees without creating noise they'd hear and follow.

"...can't pay us enough. I got a store to run."

"The reward's mighty good, if we find them. Bringin' them in for killing Mr. Ochoa like that's worth another few days of our time."

The two men argued. Dinkins hoped they were alone. Then other voices joined in the argument. From what he could tell, they were less incensed about their marshal being cut down than they were about the bank president ending up in a boneyard. Dinkins closed his eyes. He was responsible for both deaths. From the angry words being exchanged, they'd hang him twice if they figured out how to do it.

At least they weren't bragging to one another how they'd recovered the gold or caught the other robbers. After what stretched to forever, the posse moved on. The best Dinkins could tell, they worked their way downhill away from him. If he kept going in the direction he headed, the forests would thin out and he might even find himself in snow that stayed on the highest mountain tops all year long. He needed a heavy coat to survive that route.

He slowly trailed the posse back down the slope, careful not to override them.

"Other tracks," he said softly. "They wanted to follow the 'other hoofprints.'" While those might belong to anyone traveling in the Sangres, he had the feeling the posse had bypassed the trail left by his partners.

He had nothing to lose finding out. If some others meandered through these hills, he might join them and give himself some cover should the posse stumble across him.

Dinkins dropped to the ground and studied some broken limbs on a low-growing bush. Sap still oozed. He wiped the sticky goo off on his pants leg. Whoever had come this way had done so recently. And a few drops of blood hinted that a rider had been injured more severely than a light scratch from a thorn.

Walking quickly he worked his way through a dense stand of trees. A trail of blood kept him moving. Once, he heard movement and spun, hand going to his six-gun. Yellow eyes glared at him from shadow. A wolf or perhaps a coyote also followed the blood trail. Dinkins walked faster now, almost running. If the tree limbs hadn't been so low he would have ridden. As it was, he constantly ducked low branches.

He froze again when someone called his name.

"Who's there? Is that you, Wilson?" Dinkins hardly recognized the voice.

"Me. I ... it's me." The hoarse whisper warned him his partner wasn't far away—and that he was in bad shape.

Dinkins saw a larger splotch of blood staining dried leaves and went in that direction. He almost stepped on the wounded man. Wilson had covered himself with a fallen tree limb. The leaves provided good camouflage if anyone glanced in this direction.

"What happened? Where are the others?" He pulled the branch with its leaves away. Trying not to show his true thoughts, he opened Wilson's unbuttoned vest. The man's shirt was drenched with more blood than Dinkins thought could ever be in a single man's body.

Wilson saw his expression.

"Ain't all mine. Most of it is, but not all." He moaned. Dinkins supported him and cradled his head in his arms.

"Where are the others?"

"You mean what happened to the gold?" Wilson coughed up blood. He turned his head and a gobbet dribbled down his chin onto the leafy forest floor.

Dinkins saw no reason to lie.

"Did the others take the gold?"

Wilson nodded weakly and said, "The Chandlers, they, they tried to make off with it. They put another bullet in me."

"Was Randall in it with them, the dirty double-crossers?"

"He shot them. Both. They tried to kill him, too, and keep it all for themselves."

Dinkins waited for the man to tell the rest. There had to be more to the story.

"He t-tried to k-kill me, too. No matter I was already dyin'. Stone cold killer, Randall. A real skunk. But I showed him."

"You shot him first?"

"He got me a couple more times 'fore I fired back. I got lucky." Wilson tapped a spot just above his heart. "Drilled him right there. But he got away. All the gold. He ... he ..."

Dinkins dropped Wilson to the ground. The man had robbed his last bank and taken his last bullet.

He scooted back and stood. There wasn't any call burying Wilson. Let the posse find him and take the body back to Taos for a reward. That might be enough to get them off his trail.

His and Randall's.

Wilson hadn't been too specific about where the shootout with the Chandler brothers and Randall had happened but from the man's condition, it wasn't far off. Dinkins was surprised that his partner—his former partner—had gone more than a few feet with so many bullets in him. The blood loss was enough to lay low a grizzly bear.

He slowly backtracked Wilson's blood trail. Before he reached the spot where he had picked up the trail initially, he saw considerable blood. The wild animals had beaten him to it and lapped up enough. Following this new gory trail, he quickly heard snarling and snapping as animals fought over a meal.

He identified the Chandler brothers by their clothing. The coyotes hadn't left much flesh on face or belly. Dinkins circled the area, saw where Wilson had dragged himself away. The only other trail leading from the carnage went due south. That had to be Randall's trail.

He mounted and rode.

A smile of satisfaction crossed his lips when the amount of blood increased. Randall had been as badly wounded as Wilson. That kept him from making a quick getaway. All Dinkins had to do was keep on the trail and the gold would be his.

"WHY ISN'T HE DEAD?" DANDY DAN DINKINS GRUMBLED as he walked along. More than one patch of blood showed where Pete Randall had bled profusely. Anyone this seriously wounded should have had the good sense to die. "I've got a bullet just for you," he said as he came to a long stretch of rock where the blood drops were the size of silver dollars.

Randall had killed both Chandler brothers and leaving Wilson to die was his fault, too, though Dinkins had intended to finish off the trio himself. And Randall. When he had partnered up with them down in Santa Fe he had intended to rob the bank, split the take and then hightail it for Colorado. If there hadn't been such a ferocious gunfight, that was how he intended the robbery to go.

But whoever had cut down the bank president had unleashed hell. It was only through luck that he had evaded the posse this long. For all he knew, they still hunted him, though it had been close to five days now. No marshal kept a posse out that long unless he had a powerful hatred gnawing at his gut.

Dinkins shook his head. If the banker hadn't been killed, the Taos marshal wouldn't have opened fire and he wouldn't have shot him down.

"Randall," he muttered. "You're responsible for all this. It's only fair that I take the gold. All of it." There hadn't been any question that Randall had gunned down the brothers and taken all the gold. What had happened to Wilson was a mystery. It was possible he slipped away from Randall when the Chandlers were being shot in the backs. Or it could be like the dying man had said. Randall had double-crossed them all.

He touched the six-shooter in its holster. How had Randall survived such terrible wounds? It must be that a man that ornery and tough required extra lead. Dinkins was just the man to contribute an ounce or two more of lead to the double-crossing snake's gut.

He left the woods and stood in the middle of a road. Wherever it went, it wasn't well travelled but whenever a wagon happened along, it was heavily laden. The first thought he had was that the road led to a lumbering site. Dinkins walked a few yards before he saw the battered sign: High Lonesome Ice Company.

"You've got to be holed up there," he said with some satisfaction. Not giving up in his quest to recover the bank loot had paid off. It had taken him long enough to track Randall down.

He stepped up into the saddle and rode slowly, keeping a careful lookout for trouble. This was as close to other people as he'd gotten since he left Wilson and the Chandler brothers for the coyotes. All he needed was a glimpse of Pete Randall and he'd be sitting pretty. The entire time on the trail he had gone over the robbery in his head. There had to be ten thousand dollars in gold. Maybe more. That would put him in clover for a good, long time.

But not here. After he settled the score with Randall and had all that shiny gold jingling in his saddlebags, he was off to Mexico with its decent tequila and bevies of Mexican girls willing to do about anything he asked. He'd have money like a patrón and would spend it lavishly.

When he spotted a three-story building, he drew rein and studied the layout. He had come up far enough on the mountain that the ice mining went on nearby in the large barnlike structure. The freight wagon that had left the deep tracks in the road was parked beside it. Not far away a stable held at least four animals. From the sounds reaching him, mules were stabled there. And a fair sized house across the weed-overgrown yard completed the scene.

He considered what to do. A thin curl of white smoke rose from the house's chimney. The house had some occupants. A horse tied up outside nervously tugged at its reins. Dinkins tried to remember what Randall had ridden. He couldn't, not exactly, but this wasn't the same horse. He didn't think it was, at any rate, but the back shooter might have stolen another horse in the past few days. Randall's trail leading here was different from the one Dinkins had taken.

He knew the house was occupied. But how many were inside? Having someone come up behind him while he held

Randall at gunpoint was too dangerous a risk to take. He rode quietly to the icehouse to scout it out. If workers moved their blocks of ice, they'd be inside.

Dinkins drove his heels into his horse's flanks when he heard hoofbeats behind him on the road. He put the icehouse between him and the four riders approaching on the road before they spotted him.

He cursed a blue streak. A badge gleamed on the lead rider's chest. A lawman.

"Get on over to yonder house and see if anyone's been by," the deputy sheriff called to a pair of his men. "Be real careful. From the blood trail, he's wounded pretty bad."

"He'll fight like a trapped rat," another said. A smaller badge caught sunlight. Dinkins thought this was a deputy, too, but not with the sheriff's office. A deputy marshal from Taos? He and another rider without a badge trotted to the house.

"You see what's in the stables, Ned," the deputy sheriff said to the remaining posse member. "I'll give the icehouse a once over."

Dinkins touched the Colt at his side. Ambushing the law dog would be as easy as pie. The only trouble was that the other three were spread out. There wasn't any chance to bring them down, too, without a heated gunfight. He rode closer to a door on the side of the icehouse, bent and tugged to get it open.

Barred.

He had thought he might sneak inside and hide. Randall had to be here somewhere. If he let the posse catch the other robber, the gold would be lost. He backed away and looked up at the structure. A loft door two-stories above swung to and fro in the gentle breeze, but he had no way to get in.

The deputy sheriff's hollow hoofbeats came closer. Dinkins almost drew. He could ambush the law dog.

Not ready for the fight that had to follow such a murder, Dinkins turned his horse downhill and made his way into a thickly wooded patch just in time to hide. The lawman poked around, tried the door and found it barred just as Dinkins had, then continued around the building. He never even glanced downslope where Dinkins hid.

A thousand thoughts ran through Dinkins' mind. As much as he wanted revenge on Randall and to recover the gold from the bank, he wanted to keep from getting his neck stretched even more. He had seen more than one outlaw do the mid-air two-step. That wasn't going to be his fate. Not with tequila and señoritas waiting for him south of the border.

Reluctantly, he rode deeper into the forest and began using all his wiles to hide his trail. As long as he was free, a chance remained for him to recover the gold. If the posse caught Randall and took him back to Taos, he might rescue him along the road.

Rescue him and the gold. It would be a real bloodbath, but everything about the robbery so far had been. What were the additional deaths of four lawmen and his conniving partner? Recovering the gold would be worth all their lives and more.

2

Augustus Crane moved slowly. His joints hurt like hellfire this morning, but his fingers gripped the courier-delivered envelope firmly. Bright blue eyes fixed on the precise handwriting. There wasn't a return address on the letter. As postmaster for the city of Denver, that should have created a bit of scorn. Protocol had to be followed or ... why bother?

Still—

The last letter in his name—Crane—was curiously written, a double stroke used to make the E stand out.

"E for emergency," he said under his breath.

"What's that? I can't hear you when you mumble." His assistant, Bernard, came from the backroom, a stack of letters clutched in his hands. He dropped one, bent to pick it up and dropped a half dozen more. Working to gather them all up took several more seconds filled with curses.

"You don't tell me how to talk, you young whippersnapper," Crane snapped. "I tell you. Don't swear. Postal patrons might overhear you."

"Ain't nobody here, Mr. Crane," Bernard said, clutching

the stack of letters to his chest. One or two threatened to fall again, but he contorted himself to hang onto the lot.

Crane ignored his assistant and held up the letter. The envelope was plain, so common that it was available at any cut-rate stationer anywhere in the country. Anyone seeing it would never know it contained anything important.

"So, did you want something, Mr. Crane? If not I have a mountain of mail to sort. That new kid you hired to deliver's not working hard enough. If he doubled the letters delivered in a day, it wouldn't make much of a dent in the backlog."

"I'll hire another mailman," Crane said absently. He took a folding knife from his pocket, opened it and sliced open the envelope in a single deft move. He drove the point of the knife into the nicked wood counter in front of him.

"So that's how those holes got there," Bernard said. He came over and ran his fingertips over a half dozen other holes. Moving around, he avoided touching the knife left sticking upright in the wood.

"Sand them out later," Crane said. He unfolded the single sheet taken from the envelope. With a couple quick swipes, he moved his fingers lightly over the stationery. It was familiar—another part of the identification. It felt like a dollar bill because it was written on the same paper used to print US currency.

Whoever sent these letters, and Crane had his suspicions based on the paper and precision of the writing, commanded vast resources. He read the script quickly, then reread it more slowly to be sure he fully understood. Usually the information contained was of a general nature and easily acted upon. Not this time.

"Bernard, fetch a parcel from the backroom. It'll be addressed to Horatio A. Bridge with Tom McAulay in the return address."

"That just came in," Bernard said.

"You remembered it? Why?" Crane ran his fingers over his thick, gray-shot mustache.

"You know the poem. 'Horatio at the Bridge' written by Thomas McAulay? A parcel and those names? Curious."

"You've been goofing off again."

"What? I never—"

"Reading when you should be working'll get you fired. Get the parcel. Now!"

Augustus Crane waited for his assistant to vanish into the back before he crumpled the letter and envelope, then dropped the paper onto the counter. A quick move brought out a lucifer from his coat pocket. The match flared brightly when he dropped it onto the letter and envelope. Only ash remained when Bernard returned with a small parcel.

His assistant glared at the burnt spot on the counter. Not only were the holes from Crane's knife to be sanded out, now he had a section of charred wood to tend, also. Without a word, he passed over the parcel.

"I'll deliver it personally," Crane said. He hefted the brown-paper wrapped package. Many of the special delivery wood boxes were of equal weight. A few sheets of paper and perhaps an artifact or two. That's all that'd fit inside. He guessed that the box only guaranteed the integrity of the enclosed documents. Water or other destructive forces along the road from Washington, D.C. were held at bay.

"Why not hire that second postman?" Bernard asked.

"Tend the counter. And sort the mail faster." Crane grumbled more to himself as he grabbed his bowler hat and left by the front door.

He ran into a customer and bounced off, never breaking stride.

"Gus, wait, I got a bone to pick with you." The well-dressed man reached out to grab Crane by the shoulder.

The postmaster deftly ducked and dodged. His arthritis

caused a tinge in his joints. He ignored the small, dancing needles of pain.

"See Bernard. He'll take care of you, Mr. Bryant."

"I wanted to ask you—" The man spoke to Augustus Crane's back.

Crane walked as fast as he could down Marion Street, turned away from the Capitol building and located the street that led to his destination. The house he sought was imposing. A stick-style Victorian mansion, it dominated the entire area. Closer examination showed armor plate under the facade. The flagstone walk to the broad porch was guarded by a white picket fence.

He sucked in his gut, settled his nerves and made his way up the steps to the front door. Stained glass showed a bison's head on one side and a rampant buckhorn on the other.

The Society of Buckhorn and Bison. The well-lettered sign above the door was obvious. And mysterious.

He yanked on the doorbell. Somewhere deep in the bowels of the hulking house a chime sounded. Augustus Crane took a half step back in preparation for what he knew would happen. Before the chime fell silent, the door opened silently on well-oiled hinges.

"Good afternoon, sir. Do you wish to see Mr. Legende?" The butler stood a head taller than Crane's five-foot-eight and, unlike the postmaster, was impeccably dressed. His dark brown hair was carefully combed. How he shaved so close was a little frightening to Crane. It required the use of an impossibly sharp razor and deft strokes. For all the times he had delivered parcels to the Society, he had never seen so much as a stubble on Kingston's jutting, strong chin.

Crane looked at the parcel he clutched so fiercely. The fancy lettering around the E in his name on the envelope he had burned told him this was a special delivery. Normally, he handed the parcel to Kingston to be delivered to his employer.

"I have to see him this time, Kingston."

The butler silently stepped back and held the door.

"In the library, Gus," came the distant directions echoing down a long hall.

Crane glanced at the butler. Kingston silently closed the door and held out his hand to direct his visitor to the proper room. To Crane, anything away from the foyer confused him. The house was a maze of doors and corridors. And this was only the first floor. He had always wondered what the upper two stories were like.

Allister Legende met him at the library door and ushered him into the room. A marble-topped table near a bay window was flanked by two wingtip chairs. On the table within reach of someone sitting in the right-hand chair was a brandy snifter with a few sips of amber liquid remaining. Legende had been reading the book carefully marked with a red grosgrain ribbon and placed on the table next to the snifter.

"Sorry to interrupt your studies," Crane said. "The letter was marked as an emergency." He held out the paper-wrapped parcel.

Legende took the package, bounced it a couple times to judge its weight, then said, "May I interest you in a drink?"

Crane licked his lips. Legende always had the finest wines, the best whiskey, the greatest of everything.

"Please, Gus. A few more minutes won't matter to delivering mail throughout Denver."

"You talked me into it, you silver-tongued fox."

Legende slapped him on the back and said, "That's what I like to hear. Come. Sit. It's been too long since we socialized." He indicated the chair opposite his reading chair.

By the time Crane sank into it, Kingston had arrived with a cut crystal glass filled with what had to be bourbon from the aroma reaching Crane's bulbous nose. The butler held out the silver tray and waited.

The postmaster tried not to grab the glass, but he was beguiled by the reflections off the crystal and the opportunity to sample something he'd never in a hundred years be able to afford on his own.

"That's Frank Landry's stock," Legende said, distracted by opening the package.

He ripped away the paper and revealed a small, polished wood box. With a dextrous move, he slid his thumbnail under the lip and released the hidden catch. It popped open. Crane tried not to strain to see what was inside. Usually he never saw the box opened.

Legende drew out a letter. Without even running it between his fingers, Crane knew the paper was identical to that of the letter he had received. Stroke over it, think of money. Legende only glanced at the terse note and laid the letter aside. He held up a newspaper clipping. The paper's masthead was glued onto the article.

"The Las Vegas Optic?" Crane blurted out the question before he realized he was spying and shouldn't have revealed it. Discretion was a big part of his job—a job he was paid handsomely for in addition to the salary he received as postmaster.

"I remember seeing a similar story in the Rocky Mountain News," Legende said distantly. He closed his eyes for a moment, then opened them. "How is your bourbon? Mr. Landry assures me it is Mudflats Distilling's finest product."

"It goes down smooth and warms me all the way down to my toes," Crane said with real appreciation. He licked his lips to remove the lingering taste. Not even in his dreams had he sampled a better whiskey, and he had some mighty fine dreams.

"It does, indeed," Legende said. He picked up the letter,

turned it over and hunted through his pockets until he found a pencil stub. He scribbled a few words, then handed the sheet to Crane.

"Do I mail this back? I don't have an address. Or a name," he said. Augustus Crane realized how little he knew of how the Society of Buckhorn and Bison operated. He didn't even know who sent him the letters. What he did know was that at any time a dozen or more parcels rested on his warehouse shelves, each with a strange name. Most would never be delivered. Every few months a letter arrived detailing how the unclaimed packages were to be destroyed.

That was against postal regulations. He was paid so much by the Washington benefactor that he took the risk of ever being discovered. The packages with new names would begin arriving. And occasionally the letter came to let him know which one of a dozen or more to deliver to Allister Legende.

"Send a telegram to that address on the letter."

Crane studied the faint writing and nodded. Then he looked up. "Should I forget I ever saw this address?"

"Once the telegram is delivered, the address will change. Do you wish another drink, Gus?"

"Well," he said slowly. He wanted a second shot of the fine whiskey, but he had a 'gram to send. "I got to get on my way." He held up the letter.

"Thank you for your promptness. Kingston will see you out." Legende leaned back in his chair. He tented his fingers and rested his chin on the tips, thinking hard.

He looked up when Kingston returned after seeing the postmaster from the house.

"What do you require of me, sir?"

"Come into the council room. I need your help." Legende rose quickly and strode from the library. Kingston, not seeming to hurry, followed him closely in spite of the brisk pace.

Legende went into the next room, dominated by an oval table. A dozen chairs had been pushed in, showing no meeting had occurred here for some time. He went to the mantle where a dozen bullets were balanced on their bases.

"What do you think?" he asked the butler.

"The Society has a half dozen teams currently operating in the field," Kingston said. "It will be difficult to find anyone able to deal with whatever matter has so aroused our friend back East."

"There are two operatives in the exact spot we need," Legende said. "But they fight like cats and dogs."

"Yes, sir, oil and water," Kingston said. "That does not diminish their effectiveness."

Legende reached past the row of upright bullets and picked two others laying on their sides.

A .45 derringer and a .36 Colt Navy round.

Legende exhaled deeply and put the two bullets side by side at the edge of the mantle.

"Kingston, send a telegram to our Miss O'Connor." He tapped the mantle by the .45 cartridge and said, "Santa Fe."

"Yes, sir. And the other?"

Legende pointed to the Colt round. "Taos. This time Mr. Landry gets a pass. That will suit him just fine, but keep him in reserve, should he be needed as her assistant. Neither will like this but they knew the rules when they joined the Society of Buckhorn and Bison."

Kingston silently left. Legende stared at the two bullets and shook his head. It never got easier sending his agents on a mission. But this one? The two of them together? Without another thought, he turned and left the council room. The die was cast.

3

Emily O'Connor smiled winningly and batted her long, dark lashes at the expensively dressed man seated across from her. The mountain of poker chips in the center of the green-felt covered table represented a young fortune, but Emily paid no attention to how rich she would be after this hand. She was too good a poker player to be distracted. What mattered was playing the player, not the size of the bet.

The money was good. Winning was better.

"Miss O'Connor, you are such a lovely thing, but you are bluffing." The man stared hard at her, hoping to get a hint of what she held in her hand.

"Really, Mr. Bentley, would po' li'l ole me do a thing like that to a powerful, handsome man like you?" She batted her emerald eyes some more and widened her radiant smile. Then she touched the side of the mound of flame-red hair where a pearl was threatening to come loose. She meant to distract him. His eyes remained locked on hers.

She had worked all night to develop such a quick touch of

her hair as a tell for running a bluff. Bentley showed no sign that he had picked up on her carefully orchestrated show.

Emily changed her tactics and bent forward over the table, just enough to give him a flash of snowy white breasts barely constrained by her emerald silk dress. The color of that dress matched her eyes perfectly. It had taken months for her to find not only the proper cloth but the expert seamstress in St. Louis who could make the revealing gown exactly to her instructions.

The way she moved now distracted him. His eyes flickered lower, then back, but she saw the determination had fled from his expression. Lust replaced it. She wanted to tell him he was going to be doubly disappointed. Not only would he lose the pot but he stood no chance at all of fulfilling the fleeting fantasy about her.

"All I have is a thousand dollars. Oh, my," she said, shaking her head slightly as if in consternation. "Whatever will I do if I lose it all?"

"You're folding?" He still glanced at her breasts but tried not to be obvious.

"Oh, no, I'm betting it all. Every last penny." She pushed it forward to create a veritable Pike's Peak of black poker chips in the center of the table.

"You run a good bluff, madam, but I must call you." He turned over a full house, treys full of jacks. He reached for the pot.

"What a fine hand," she said.

Bentley's eyes snapped off the money to lock with hers. Emily's tone froze him like stone.

She dropped four queens onto the table. Silence fell on the room.

"My favorite hand," she said brightly. "Those lovely ladies always keep me company when I need them the most." She gestured to a liveried servant standing to one side of the card-room. With slow elegance she pointed to the greenbacks and poker chips piled up like Pike's Peak on the table. "Please see to them for me, will you, Pablo?"

The man repressed a grin. Before the game Emily had spoken at length with all the servants to find out as much about the invited guests as possible. Pablo was a reticent man, hesitant to speak about those who visited the governor in his mansion, but she had coaxed a considerable flood of information about Bentley from him. The elegantly dressed man, for all his apparent manners, was not well considered by any of the staff.

"You are the lucky one tonight, Miss O'Connor," Bentley said stiffly. He obviously forced himself to be cordial.

"And you are not, Mr. Bentley." She flashed an even wider smile as she pushed back from the table. "All this card play has built a thirst worthy of your vast and arid New Mexico desert."

The other men at the table scrambled to stand. Two looked anxious that she would accompany them and one didn't. And then there was Bentley, now glaring at her as she sifted through the money she had won. She made a point of handing Pablo five hundred dollars in greenbacks and saying sotto voce, "Be a dear and divide this among the staff, will you, sir? Thank you."

She gathered the remainder of the money, hefting a heavy leather pouch with the gold coins, and slipped into the next room where a twelve-foot long mahogany bar polished to a mirror finish dominated the entire north wall.

"You seem to be the winner this evening," a small, slender man with a thin black mustache said. He wore clothing suitable for an audience with the President. Not a speck of dust marred the midnight black coat or the aggressively polished hand-tooled boots. A thick gold watch chain swung about as he moved. The heavy watch was swallowed up in the pocket of the lily-white vest fastened with ebony buttons. As far as Emily could see, the man wasn't armed. But then, in this place, there was no call for him to pack even a hideout popper.

"It seems so, Governor," she said, inclining her head in his direction. "It's so nice of you to invite me to your home."

"The door to the Palace of the Governors is always open to you, Miss O'Connor." He bowed slightly. "Let my assistant cash in your chips. You have cornered the market in them, as well as scrip and coins. I should hire you as my chancellor of the exchequer." He gestured and a tall, slender man who had watched them like a circling Harris hawk glided forward.

"Thank you," she said. She took an instant dislike to the governor's right-hand man and couldn't decide why until she saw him exchange a knowing look with Bentley. The gent she had just cleaned out at poker and the governor's assistant were in cahoots.

Business? Politics? If the latter, the governor wasn't long for his position.

"A drink, my dear." The governor held out his arm and escorted her to a small table with two comfortable chairs.

By the time they'd seated, drinks were placed in front of them.

"You are quite observant, Governor." She held up the cut crystal glass filled with two fingers of bourbon.

"I am sure you appreciate a fine whiskey, but you should sample my tequila. I have it shipped in monthly from Mexico." He curled a single brown finger around his glass of amber fluid.

"Do you drink it with salt and lime?"

"As much as I have learned of you, Miss O'Connor, you continue to surprise me. Are you truly from Boston?" He laughed lightly. "No, getting the lime is difficult at this time of year. In a few months ..." He shrugged expressively.

"If Santa Fe enjoyed more trade, perhaps getting such fruits would be easier throughout the year."

"Trade? You speak of trade?" His eyes narrowed. "Do you represent such a company willing to freight agricultural products? There are already several companies shipping goods through my capital."

"Ah, Governor, they all come through Raton Pass, after going by Bent's Fort. If freighters came through Texas from the Gulf Coast ports, many new products would be available."

"Such a trading license is expensive," he said.

"Difficult to obtain, also," she said, smiling. "Unless there is a powerful man backing such a franchise."

"Such a powerful man who now lacks lime for his tequila? You are empowered to make such a contract, Miss O'Connor?"

"Oh, dear me, no. I am but a messenger for those who can. At this moment in Galveston is a ship bulging with citrus fruits from Central and South America."

"This cargo can be shipped here? In spite of the Comanches and Navajos? In spite of the route being so accurately called *Jornado del Muerto*?"

"No territorial militia would be required," she said. "All that you need do is—" Emily looked over her shoulder, her lips thinning in anger at being interrupted. The governor was close to agreeing to a trade agreement that would prove quite lucrative for not only New Mexico Territory but the Texas merchants who had employed her negotiating skills.

Her commission on the first shipment would finance a year of high stakes poker at San Francisco's Union Club. She might even venture back to Boston to see about the most *au courant* fashions from Paris and Milan.

"Miss O'Connor." Pablo tugged at her sleeve now.

"You're wrinkling the silk," she snapped. Then she calmed herself. "*Lo siento*, Pablo. What is so important?"

The servant looked over at the governor. The politician was similarly irritated at the interruption. Pablo took a deep breath and said in a rush, "There is a telegram of great importance."

"I'll see to it—" She bit off her words. "Who is it from?"

"The Society."

She stared at him, her emerald eyes unblinking. The only way Pablo would have interrupted her talk with the governor, no matter how urgent the telegram, was if he knew about the Society.

The Society of Buckhorn and Bison.

Emily never questioned the possibility that Pablo had a bullet standing upright on Allister Legende's mantle in the council room. He might be less than a full member, but he knew details even highly placed politicians did not. He knew and that was good enough for her.

"Governor, I must see to this matter. Excuse me."

"But Miss O'Connor—Emily!"

She left him sucking air. The contract to ship produce from Texas was no longer possible to negotiate, she knew. But Legende had no reason to track her down and send a telegram unless the matter was vital.

"Here, Señorita O'Connor." Pablo pointed to a vaquero holding a flimsy yellow paper envelope. He hardly looked the sort to carry common messages. Rather she saw him in all his finery, from the elaborate sombrero with ornate silver designs threaded over the crown down to his fancy tooled boots as owning a rancho. This only added to the urgency.

She ripped open the envelope and held it up to a candle mounted in a wall sconce. After reading it a second time, she touched the corner of the thin paper to the flame. The telegram turned to ash in a split second.

"Is the lawman from Taos here in town?"

"Sheriff Thompson recruits from the local marshal's deputies for a posse," Pablo said.

"Take me to him. Immediately." She looked from Pablo to the vaquero, wondering who would be her escort.

With a broad gesture, the vaquero doffed his hat and swept it in front using a gesture she expected from British nobility.

She took her shawl from Pablo as she exited into the chilly New Mexico night. She had been to Santa Fe many times, and it always impressed her how a dusty, sleepy town had become a hub for such considerable commerce. The streets in front of the Palace of the Governors was empty except for a carriage. The vaquero helped her in.

She settled down and thought hard about the telegram. Society business. Legende demanded immediate action. She had to find whoever had killed a man in Taos named Ochoa and ...

Legende hadn't specified what had to be done. Bringing the killer to justice wasn't likely to be as simple as turning him over to the law. Something more was involved. Otherwise, the local law dogs were adequate for the chore. It wasn't as if they hadn't dealt with murderers before. This was a frontier, filled with renegades, outlaws and men so ornery they'd shoot their own shadow because it trailed them.

The carriage creaked to halt.

Emily stepped down, not waiting for the vaquero to take her hand. She lifted her long skirts and hurried into the marshal's office. The thick smoke almost made her cough. A half dozen men, all wearing badges clustered around the marshal's desk to study a map. Six sets of eyes fixed on her as she stepped inside, but only one spoke.

"Ma'am, we got an important matter to deal with. If you'd come back tomorrow—"

"I just came from the governor," she said. "He wants me to keep him informed of all the details. *All* of them."

"Tell him to come here if he—"

"Sheriff Thompson, that's his man outside. He drove here in the governor's carriage." The deputy peering out the door swallowed hard. "You've heard about Alvarez."

"The one they call El Diablo?" The sheriff sounded impressed.

Emily kept a poker face, but she was impressed, too. Not many men provoked such a hint of awe and outright respect. She had been escorted here by the governor's "fixer."

"Time is of the essence. All the details, please," she said. She wanted to get them talking, spilling facts she could use to satisfy Allister Legende's assignment.

"I'm recruiting a posse to get on over to Taos. The town marshal there was cut down during the robbery and the deputy marshal's not up to what has to be done."

"And that is?" Emily moved closer to get a better look at the map. The map showed the Sangre de Cristo Mountains from up in Colorado stretching down south of Santa Fe. Taos was clearly marked, as were several dotted lines leading from the town.

"Those are rugged mountains," Sheriff Thompson said obliquely.

Emily understood that when the posse caught the killer, he'd never be brought back to stand trial.

"What happened that the marshal was killed?"

"A bank robbery," spoke up the Santa Fe marshal. "The robbers murdered Mr. Ochoa—he was the bank president—and when Marshal Nolan came rushing up, he got hisself kilt, too."

"And the robbers?"

"They got shot up pretty bad getting away. Two were cut down by their own partners. We figured it was a double-cross.

From the blood trails, the other three are like as dead from their wounds, too."

"That's what the Taos sheriff here says." He glared at a lawman in the circle. For the first time Emily saw his badge was markedly different from the others. This was the man who had come to Santa Fe to recruit his posse rather than relying on citizens local to Taos. "I want to see the bodies before I make any claim to them being brought down." The Santa Fe marshal openly scoffed at the Taos sheriff's abilities. "The law that's left up there won't be worth two hoots and a holler."

"Why's that?"

"They're all thicker than thieves up there, not saying the lawmen there are crooked, mind you. It's just that they're hunting down their own friends."

"You watch what you say about me and my deputies," the Taos sheriff snapped. "I need your help, but I'm not willing to put up with your insults much longer."

The marshal snorted in contempt.

"Do you know the robbers, Sheriff?" Emily asked, forestalling an argument that could only waste time and might erupt into gunplay between the lawmen.

"Maybe not two of the varmints," the sheriff said, "but I sure as hell know one what got away with the gold."

"He has a name? Reporting this to the governor would go a long way toward easing his mind that you have the situation well in hand." Emily asked the question of the sheriff but studied the Santa Fe marshal since he had the grimmest expression.

As she expected, the sheriff answered. "The thief and killer we want most is called Pete Randall."

"Randall?" Emily stiffened. "Pete Randall? Are you sure?"

"He runs an ice company up in the hills, near the tree line along Ute Ridge. From accounts, nobody expected him to go bad, but he did. And it'll be up to us to catch the owlhoot."

"Peter Randall," Emily repeated softly.

"That's the one we're going to bring to hang until his damned head pops off his shoulders." The Taos sheriff's declaration was met with assent by every lawman in the room.

Emily knew Pete Randall and his wife. It couldn't be a coincidence of names. The Randalls she knew owned an ice company up in the hills, too. Allister Legende wanted justice for Jaime Ochoa's death. She hoped Pete and his wife Elizabeth weren't involved.

If she wanted to save Randall's life, she had to find her friend's husband before the law did—all the law in northern New Mexico. All the law and the Society of Buckhorn and Bison.

4

The town plaza seemed oddly quiet.

Frank Landry rode slowly past the gazebo with its peeling paint and uncomfortable warped wood plank benches and hunted for some sign of life anywhere. Taos wasn't supposed to be this dull. Everything he had heard about the northern New Mexico town told him this was the perfect place for him to branch out from his job as salesman for the Mudflats Distilling company based in Kansas City.

But he needed some sign to encourage him that he hadn't wasted his time coming here.

"We'll do just fine," he said, patting his horse, Barleycorn, on the neck. The dun-colored gelding whinnied and turned a large brown eye back toward him. He accepted the quiet scorn. The trip through Raton Pass had been difficult. The tollkeeper on the road had tried to gyp him out of every single dime riding in Frank's poke.

His usual gift of gab hadn't eased him through. That irritated him as much as anything else. It had taken a full bottle of his best bourbon, and that pushed him to the point of exploding. Passing out samples was one thing when the potential buyer was a saloon owner who would buy a couple dozen cases. When the recipient was a one-eyed, grizzled gray beard intent on robbing—legally—everyone passing by his tollbooth, that was a horse of a different color.

If it hadn't been for the man's belligerence and a pair of sons with rifles positioned in rocky redoubts, Frank would have ridden on through without paying.

"Ah, a fine looking cantina," he said, spying a sleepy looking adobe building with a small, well-lettered sign out front. "We should start there. Don't you agree, Barleycorn?"

The horse snorted in disgust. Frank was inclined to agree with such equine wisdom. Mia Tia's Cantina hardly showed the prosperous clientele entering that he usually sought. But his trip to Taos was intended to do more than make a heap big profit for Mudflats Distilling. This time he would feather his own nest with a sideline business. His bosses back East didn't have to know he was undercutting them by selling his own brand of who-hit-John distilled locally.

He stepped down, stretched and adjusted his once-black frock coat. A quick brush knocked off clouds of trail dust from both coat and vest. Then he touched the Colt Navy slung in a cross-draw holster. A quick move of his thumb slid off the leather thong over the hammer. Trouble popped up unexpectedly. Whenever he scouted a new market, it took days to learn all the pitfalls. Having the Colt close to hand reassured him that, no matter how things went against him, he'd come out on top.

A quick whip of reins around a hitch post secured his gelding. He grunted as he unfastened his sample case. Barleycorn whinnied in relief, being free of not only the rider but his heavy liquid cargo. Frank ducked under the cantina's low lintel and stood for a moment just inside the door. His eyes adjusted to the low light.

He heaved a sigh. Every time he sought a new market, he

expected something ... different. So far, his disappointment was complete. Every saloon might have been the twin of the one he just left. In New Mexico the cantinas were different only in that the ceilings were lower and the walls were three-foot thick adobe bricks. Otherwise, the bar was the same. Tables carefully placed around the interior showed beer stains and nicks on ill-kept surfaces. More than one had a bullet hole in it. And a poker game with five desultory players progressed at the rear.

If he was any judge, and he was, the men weren't professional gamblers. They gathered to pass the time with friends, arguing and disputing each others' hands more to break the monotony than to profit. Although he couldn't see the pot, he guessed it was nothing but a few pennies. A nickel bet from these players would be commented on and a dime was out of the question as being too rich for the lot of them.

"Welcome to Taos," the barkeep greeted. "What's your pizzen?"

Frank sized up the man in a flash. A rotund belly poked out the canvas apron to such an extent that it was impossible to believe the man had ever missed a meal or passed on second helpings. His round face was marked by eyebrows that grew together and a bushy mustache that once had been waxed to sharp points but now ended in twin frizzy tips. The smile was mechanical, but the eyes held Frank's attention. Nothing about those twin beacons showed dullness or weakness. This was a man who did whatever was necessary.

"Good to be greeted so warmly by the establishment owner," Frank said. He thrust out his hand. "I'm Frank Landry and I'm here to improve the quality of your liquor."

The man took Frank's hand and shook tentatively.

"You a whiskey peddler? You can save your wind. I've got all the liquor I need."

"Oh, I am sure you have tequila and rye whiskey and

perhaps even some of that Taos Lightning rumored to be about the most potent moonshine in the territory, but I have pure distilled bourbon. And I even have a sample of scotch, straight from the highlands of far-off Scotland."

"You don't listen so good, do you? I said I'm supplied."

Something in the man's words put Frank on guard. He was hinting that he not only didn't want to buy from an outsider but that he couldn't. Someone had the market in Taos all sewed up—probably with threats and a bullet or two to seal the deal.

"That interests me," he said.

"What's that?" The barkeep took a step back and cast a dark look in Frank's direction.

"The moonshine. If you introduced me to a purveyor of it, I—" Frank cut off his request. The bartender's eyes darted about, as if he sought a way to clear out.

Frank put his elbow on the bar and half turned toward the doorway. Silhouetted there was a slight man who carried a six-shooter on either hip. The number of gunslicks Frank had seen in his day who handled both guns expertly was small. Mostly men wore two six-shooters to impress the ladies or intimidate the men who refused to strap on a gun belt.

As the gunman bent slightly to avoid hitting his head and entered, a stray sunbeam glinted off a badge.

"How're you doing today, Henry?" the law dog called out to the man behind the bar.

The only answer he got was a contemptuous snort. Frank tried to figure out the power structure in Taos if the marshal was held in such low regard.

Frank waited for the marshal to notice him. It took only a second.

"I'm only saying this once, mister," he said without so much as a "howdy." His tone wasn't friendly, either, as if he offered decent advice rather than a warning. "You're a stranger in Taos and don't know how things are here."

"Learning is part of living," Frank said, trying to keep his tone light. "I'm always on the lookout for new things to inform myself."

"You asked Henry here about Taos Lightning."

"I never answered, Marshal Babson. There's no way I could, not without lyin' through my teeth. I don't know nuthin' 'bout illegal booze bein' sold."

"You're an honest soul, Henry. I know you wouldn't tell a complete stranger about illicit liquor that'd burn out his gut and make him blinder than a cave snake."

"No, sir—Marshal Babson, is it? Did I hear the name right? No, sir, Henry here was reacting to my sales pitch and nothing more. My card, sir." Frank pulled out a business card from a vest pocket and handed it to the marshal.

The man squinted as he read every word. His lips moved. Then he read it again before tucking the card into a coat pocket.

"This makes you out to be an honest whiskey peddler, Mr. Landry. Let me make it clear. Not everybody in town fancies a stranger of your occupation."

"Now, Marshal, you wouldn't be one of those temperance advocates, would you?"

"He doesn't know what he is," grumbled Henry. The barkeep pointedly turned his back on them and went to the card table and sank into an empty chair. The players bent forward and whispered furiously, occasionally glancing in Frank's direction.

"Is that true, Marshal? What's your stand on Taos Lightning?" Frank watched the young man's expression rippled like water in a fast running stream. Clearly a man in conflict about what he thought.

"I was brung up believin' that it's Satan's milk. Marshal Nolan, rest his soul, was even more opposed than I am."

"So you feel you should honor his memory by being a supporter of the temperance movement?" Frank saw this was the case, but something more fed the young man's aversion to homespun moonshine. "So you took over when Nolan was gunned down? Tell me about how that happened in such a quiet town as Taos." Frank had no interest in such things but wanted the marshal to ramble on some more. He might divulge a tidbit of useful information.

"It stirred up 'bout everyone in these parts, him gettin' shot down like he was," Babson said. "And there was more to mourn about the robbery. Mr. Ochoa was a rich fellow as well as president of the bank. Powerful politically, too. Most folks around here, well, he'd say 'frog' and they'd all jump."

"Including Nolan?"

"Especially the marshal. Him and Mr. Ochoa was raised together and were real good friends."

"So Ochoa wasn't keen on taking a nip of moonshine?"

"Can't say that he was. He claimed it hurt his freight company. He owned Sangre Freight and brought most all of what we eat here in Taos up from Santa Fe. He has a train of more than ten wagons. Well, he *had* that many. Now he don't have any, reason of bein' dead and all."

Frank pieced together the power structure. Ochoa owned the town and now both he and his enforcer—the newly deceased marshal—were gone. The power vacuum left behind hinted at bloodshed in the future until a new boss solidified his iron grip.

And with the old guard gone, that meant opportunities for advancement. Frank saw that his chance to cut himself into the making of Taos Lightning was better than it had been before the bloody bank robbery. All he needed to do was avoid wet-behind-the-ears Marshal Babson as he went about finding who ran the stills and what it'd take for them to expand their market.

"This your case? On the bar?" Babson poked it with his index finger, as if it might rear up and bite him.

"It is."

"I don't cotton much to illegal 'shine. Don't much like legal whiskey, either. Since Henry back there's not too inclined to buy from you, why don't you head on out of town? By sunup tomorrow."

"But there are other saloons," Frank protested. "This was the only the first one I came across. I haven't had a chance to—"

"Be turned down by all of them, too. Well, Mr. Landry, that's what will happen. I'll spread the word. Have a good day." The marshal touched the brim of his hat, grinned broadly and strutted out, the conquering hero for the forces of temperance in Taos.

Frank looked around at Henry, who turned his back. Such dismissal was absolute. Not wanting to waste any more time, Frank closed his case, heaved it off the bar and stalked after the marshal. The lawman had disappeared. The dusty streets wound around as if they'd been laid out by following a drunk cow. For all he knew, Babson was only around the nearest bend in the street some twenty yards distant.

"I don't think my boss back in KC is going to look kindly on total failure," he said, taking his gelding's reins and leading the horse deeper into town. "There's got to be one cantina willing to buy some finer whiskey from me."

Not setting himself up as a moonshine magnate rankled, too. But it was better to keep the powers that be at Mudflats Distilling happy than to return empty handed. Still, there was money to be had if only he found the right moonshiners.

An afternoon of inquiries led him to the conclusion that Marshal Babson had wings on his feet. Wherever Frank went, the marshal had just been there warning the saloon owner of a traveling salesman. Not able to get a decent conversation started made it impossible for Frank to learn more about who controlled the moonshine in town.

If Taos was like most places, there were several men running stills. But the potent Taos Lightning was famous—infamous!—for its potency and quality. Frank wanted to cut himself into that trade, but the possibility looked increasingly dismal.

He sank into a chair outside a large saloon and leaned back. The building was big enough to hold fifty patrons. If anywhere in Taos bought moonshine the White Elephant was it. All he had to do was sit and watch and wait. Eventually whoever concocted Taos Lightning would come by.

The sun sank fast behind the western mountains and left Frank shivering. He intended to tough it out. The saloon filled to half capacity, but it was only the middle of the week. For a Wednesday, the White Elephant had a brisk trade. But none of the patrons hurrying inside had the look he sought.

"You can freeze out here. It gets that cold at night, even in spring." The mocking voice added, "Especially in early spring when a man needs a nip of something strong enough to warm up his innards."

Frank took off his hat and stood, bowing elegantly to the young lady standing just off the boardwalk in the dusty street.

"Good evening, Miss. You words are quite true. The spring still carries an edge of winter to it."

"You don't look down on your luck. Why aren't you inside? Presbyterian John's got good liquor and the price shouldn't scare you off, not dressed as fine as you are."

"Ah, I am not sitting out here looking inside for lack of money. Or, indeed, for lack of anything to drink." He opened his case and showed the tops of six bottles.

"You do travel well, sir. Is that all intended to quench your own thirst? If so, you are drier than the desert." The woman stepped onto the wooden planks and came closer, finally giving him a decent look at her as light from inside bathed her.

He bowed even more and said, "Your beauty is so radiant no red-blooded man can ever claim to be cold in your presence."

"So you've got the hots for me?" She laughed. Frank perked up. It wasn't from contempt but interest, that laugh. "That's a more roundabout way than most around here would put it."

"I come from the big city. Up in Denver."

"And selling liquor is what brings you here," she said.

Frank studied her more closely. More meaning was carried in that single declaration than was stated outright. She knew what brought him to town.

She wore trail clothing. A long split blue denim skirt for riding. Her blouse was dark. In the light spilling from inside the saloon it was hard to tell the color, but he thought it was naturally beige and not from dust. Her dark hair was pulled back into a ponytail held by a flashing silver ring decorated with tiny slivers of turquoise.

When she smiled the night lit up. Her dark eyes puzzled him, though. They reminded him of someone else. They were almost coal-dark, so it wasn't his ex-wife's emerald green. Before he had a chance to figure out who she reminded him of, her tanned oval face and quirky lips and those eyes, she broke him out of his reminiscence.

"You're as much interested in buying liquor as you are selling it." Again she made a flat statement as if she read his very soul.

"I've been led to believe that selling moonshine is frowned on in Taos."

"By the deputy marshal." She laughed again, this time

with an even more curious undertone of mockery and—something more.

"Don't know the deputy. It was the marshal himself."

"He's the newly minted marshal," she corrected. "Jasper's fallen under the evil influence of his sweetheart."

"Who coincidentally might just head the local temperance league," Frank furnished. "You don't abide by their beliefs?"

"If you want to buy some Taos Lightning I can introduce you to a gent who makes the finest booze anywhere in the Sangre de Cristo Mountains."

"You have a personal connection?"

"You are a cautious cuss, aren't you? My relationship with Buck Isaacson is private. If you want to dig deeper, I suggest you make a fork on that horse of yours and ride on back to Denver."

"That's already been suggested by your new marshal." Frank cleared his throat. "I'd be delighted to meet your Mr. Isaacson."

"I thought you would. Come along. If you're real nice to me, I might even sweet talk Buck into letting you sample some of his latest batch. It is a pure delight as it slips on down your gullet."

She held out her arm. He looped his around and they headed away from the White Elephant into a section of Taos that looked to have been deserted by both residents and God.

5

Frank Landry considered why the woman was helping him find the moonshiner. For the moment, though, walking along the serpentine Taos streets wit a lovely lady on his arm was good enough.

"There," she said. "That's where Buck hangs his hat."

Frank looked over the adobe house. It had seen better days. Chunks of mud had been knocked free of the exterior walls. The door leading into the house hardly fit. During a windstorm or heavy snow, the inside would fill up fast due to thumb-sized cracks between around the frame and dried wood door.

"Buck's not too prosperous, is he?"

"It doesn't pay to be too obvious about your sideline in this town," she said. "He gets by." She looked at him with her unfathomable eyes and smiled crookedly. "*We* get by."

"I'm Frank Landry. What do I call you?"

"Jenny," she said, showing a delightful set of dimples now. "I like that name."

"Just Jenny?"

"I don't like the rest of my name." She stepped up and rapped sharply on the door.

The hollow sound warned Frank that the interior was in the same condition as the exterior—abandoned. He stepped back and moved to pull his Colt Navy slung in a cross-draw holster.

"Don't be so nervy, Frank." Jenny knocked again. The same drum noise echoed about the structure. This time the door creaked open.

The man inside was cloaked in shadow. He poked his head out and looked up and down the street, then stared hard at Frank.

"Who's this?"

"A gent who talks a big game. But he probably has big money to buy some Lightning."

"Jenny says you make the best. Is that true?"

"Get inside. The marshal's been on the prowl lately." The man glared at Jenny, as if this was her fault.

Frank wondered if it was. Jenny was open about telling a complete stranger how to buy moonshine. Her glib nature might have caused the young marshal to come after her friends—or associates. He tried to figure out the relationship between the dark-haired woman and the man scuttling about in the tiny room like a rat.

The moonshiner had a furtive look that went beyond hiding in such a wreck of a house. A blanket had been tossed over a pile of straw where he slept. A single coal oil lamp stood on a rickety chair to provide all the light inside. Other than those items, the room was bare.

"You got money to spend? We got Taos Lightning enough to float a China Clipper."

"I'm not sure how much I can sell," Frank said. "I have connections down in Santa Fe to move ten gallons a week."

"A week?" Jenny gasped. The man silenced any further outcry with a cold look.

"Depending on the price, maybe more. I'll need to contact my partners farther south in Albuquerque and over at Fort Union." He dropped that hint to see how serious Jenny and her partner were about selling him the 'shine. Given a big enough quantity, he could freight it around New Mexico Territory and garner a decent profit selling out the rear of a wagon.

The man shook his head. "There's no way you can move a drop of booze at an Army post. A soldier caught drinking on duty gets ten lashes and turned out."

"I don't condone drinking on duty. Off duty, though ..." Frank Landry let the words trail off.

"You have a sutler willing to sell to the soldiers?" The man shook his head. "I've tried for months to get somebody at the fort to sell my 'shine."

"Connections are important," Frank said. He learned a great deal from what the man said. Fort Union had been a possible market, but he thought his time would be better spent finding others.

"You rode into town all by your lonesome. You'll need a wagon to move ten gallons."

"You're getting ahead of yourself," Frank said. He glanced at Jenny. Her face vanished in shadow but from the set of her lush body she wasn't too happy with her partner. It was as if she found the buyers and her associate only made the moonshine. Frank assumed this was Buck Isaacson, but without an introduction it might be someone else.

"What do you mean? You said you wanted ten gallons." The man stepped back and moved toward a six-gun shoved into his waistband. "You're not gonna back out on our deal."

"Tell him, Jenny. There hasn't been a deal yet. We haven't dickered on the price, and I'm not sure you even have a drop of good 'shine. After all, you haven't offered me a taste of what you claim is prime Taos Lightning,"

"I don't know you've got any money, either!"

"Don't pull the iron," Frank said sharply. "We're still stepping lightly here. There's no call to threaten each other."

"He's right, Buck. We're just making a little chin music." Jenny crossed her arms and looked at Frank. He wished her face was illuminated by the pitiful lamp light.

"Why are you takin' his side?" Buck demanded.

"Because I know he has the money. I saw his wad back at the saloon."

Frank blinked. She was lying. He hadn't flashed any greenbacks, and she hadn't been inside. The first time he'd seen her was when she approached him outside the White Elephant.

"It seems you are the perfect go-between, Jenny. You know I have the money and you know that Buck here has the 'shine. What do you say we go somewhere and discuss the matter further?"

"Somewhere you can sample the 'pot liquor?'" She laughed at the little joke.

"Who knows how long it might take? Do you have a place? Or is this it?" Frank kept his eyes on Buck as he swept his left arm in an arc to indicate the dingy room.

"This is our office."

"Where you do business," Frank said caustically.

"I don't see you havin' any fancy ass place of business, mister. You're nothin' but a travelin' peddler who—" Buck cut off in mid sentence.

Both he and Jenny looked toward the door. For a second Frank wondered what spooked them. Then he heard the scraping as someone lifted the door up to open it without alerting anyone inside.

Buck dived for the blanket-covered straw pallet in the back corner and began digging like a prairie dog. A trapdoor in the floor groaned as he opened it. And like a frightened prairie dog, he dived down. Frank heard him scuttling away down a tunnel.

Jenny tugged on his arm.

"That way gets you out. Go on." Her fingernails dug into his flesh.

"You go," Frank said. He pushed her toward the hole. "I can talk my way out of anything."

"It's the marshal. I can—"

"Go!" Frank gave her a second shove, grabbed for the coal oil lamp and caught it by the base just as the door was flung open.

With an underhand throw, he tossed the hurricane lamp. It smashed against the doorframe. The volatile liquid sloshed all over. When the still-burning wick touched it, the dry wood exploded like a stick of dynamite. Bits of glass blasted back toward him, cutting exposed flesh as fiery sparks tried to ignite his clothing.

"Fire!" he yelled. He lowered his head and ran like a charging bull from the building. Creating as much confusion as possible only aided him in getting away.

He crashed into the marshal. The two of them became entangled. Arms and legs flailing about Frank crashed to the dusty street with the lawman weighing him down. They struggled, and Frank finally pushed the marshal back to the ground, face grinding into the dirt.

Wasting no time, he sprinted down the street. Lead flew past him as he ran.

"Stop or I'll fill you with lead, you mangy varmint!" Marshal Babson pounded after him.

Frank had no idea where to hide. The twisting streets confused him. Any of them might lead to a dead end—and his end. He turned a corner, saw a wall around a house built in typical Spanish fashion. He got a running start and jumped.

His fingers caught the top of the wall. When he had enough of a grip, he pulled himself up and laid flat along the thick adobe. In the courtyard dogs barked. They sounded vicious. If he'd continued, he would be ripped apart.

But he wasn't able to drop back to the street. Babson stalked along, reloading as he came.

"Give up and I promise not to kill you."

Frank had heard better deals in his day. Snarling, snapping dogs on one side and the law dog on the other, he pressed himself as flat as possible. In the dark, the marshal couldn't see him from the street. But the dogs! They smelled his fear.

Babson walked on, giving Frank a chance to slip away. He got to his feet, took a few seconds to balance, and walked slowly along the dried mud pathway. The red-tiled roof of the house stretched away from the street in one direction. To land there would cause a commotion loud enough to wake the dead. He had another way to escape.

He waited for the lawman to disappear into the night and jumped back to the street. He retraced his route to the house. Finding it in the dark was easy. It was the only one with a burned doorway.

Frank ducked inside and found where he had set down his case with the liquor samples. A quick check showed that Jenny had pulled the straw and blanket back to hide the trapdoor. He smiled. She had escaped.

He returned to the doorway and froze. The marshal stood, six-shooter drawn and pointed at his midriff.

"I reckoned you were the one here."

"I was only looking for a place to spend the night, Marshal. Taos doesn't have too many hostels open this time of night."

"We got plenty of cathouses."

"I meant—never mind. Why are you stroking that trigger like you mean to shoot me? I haven't done anything."

"Come along. I'm not sure what you're up to, but I want you where I can keep an eye on you." The marshal plucked Frank's Colt Navy from his holster.

"A nice hotel?"

"Yeah, a real nice place. It's got a cot and if you sweet talk me, you might even get breakfast before you hit the trail in the morning. Where's your horse?"

"Back at the White Elephant, I suspect," Frank said. "If I climb up on my trusty horse right now, can I ride on out and save you fixing that breakfast for me?"

Marshal Babson gestured with his pistol. Frank shrugged. It had been worth a try. He and the lawman hadn't gotten off to a good start. Now that careless animosity came back to bedevil him. They walked along twisting, turning streets and came to the plaza.

"There," Babson said. "But you likely know that's the jail. You and iron bars ain't strangers, unless I miss my guess. One might even say you have an affinity for gettin' yourself locked up in a cage. Ain't that right?"

"My horse," Frank said, blinking. Barleycorn was tethered to the side of the calaboose.

"I need to figure out what size of fine you need to pay. It's possible your horse, and a mighty fine one it is, too, and all that tack might just about cover it."

Frank tensed. As he did, the marshal slugged him.

"Get in there. To show what a nice fellow I am, you can choose which cell to occupy."

Three cells made from two-inch wide black strips riveted into cages all looked unappealing. He took the one in back.

"A good choice." Babson shoved him inside and secured the heavy lock on the door.

"Is there room service?" Frank immediately regretted trying to joke. The look on the marshal's face showed a deadly streak pushing its way to the surface.

"Why are you so downright cantankerous?" Frank asked. "I'm an honest businessman. You may not like the product I sell, but it's legal. All the taxes are paid on every bottle. It's not like this Taos Lightning I heard so much about. No taxes, sold under the table."

"My good friend got gunned down in a bank robbery."

"The former marshal?"

"And about the most important man in town, too. The bank president was murdered by the robbers."

"I have never tried to rob a bank. Not ever."

"Your morals are in question. I don't know you, and you come breezin' into town right after Jaime is murdered."

"That was the bank president?"

"He was a good man. About the finest in Taos."

"Again, I had nothing to do with killing him. Or the marshal. I—"

Frank's mouth turned to cotton. The jailhouse door opened and a familiar figure entered.

"Good evening, Jasper," she greeted.

"What're you doing out so late, Jenny?" The marshal went to the woman and hugged her. "You should be home in bed all safe and sound."

"I heard gunshots and worried about you."

"Everything's under control." Babson turned and stared pointedly at Frank. Behind his back, Jenny winked broadly and waved.

What had he gotten himself into?

6

"You have a visitor, I see," Jenny said. "What's he locked up for?"

"Mopery with intent to lurk," the marshal said. "I'll think of something more serious later on. He's up to no good. I know it deep down in my bones. Right now, I want him where I can keep an eye on him."

"He's certainly worth looking at," she said. Jenny gave him a sultry look and her tongue crept out to make a slow circuit of her ruby, bow-shaped lips.

If the marshal saw that look, he'd shoot his prisoner and horsewhip the woman.

"Jenny, you hush up. That's no way for a married woman to talk." Babson put his arm around her waist and pulled her close to plant a kiss on her cheek. She shied away.

"Oh, Jasper, behave yourself. We're in public. Or at least we're in front of your prisoner." She disengaged the marshal's arm around her and came to the cell. Every step was as sinuous as a cat stalking its prey and twice as suggestive.

Frank held his breath. He had stepped into quicksand,

and now it was sucking him under. He had no idea what to say to the woman who had taken him to buy illegal hootch.

"So what's your name, stranger?" She made it sound dirty the way she asked.

He told her. "And you're Mrs. Babson?"

"How clever of you to figure that out. The marshal's my loving hubby."

"Too bad you don't share the same interests," Frank said before he could stop himself.

"What do you mean?" The marshal barked the question from across the room.

Jenny hid her face from her husband. Her grin was positively wicked.

"Oh, dear, he doesn't mean anything. He's your prisoner. You have him all locked up, and he wants to be free to do his ... *things*."

"Reckon that's true. You get away from him, Jenny. He might be dangerous. I don't want you gettin' hurt none, especially by the likes of a whiskey peddler."

"Did he shoot at you?"

"He ran from me. Or I think he did. Whoever I chased from that abandoned building got clean away after flingin' a lit lamp at me. I doubled back to that house on Calle Espejo. You know the one?"

"You think whoever lives there is selling moonshine? I know the spot. You caught him there?"

"He was inside after he set fire to the place." Babson brightened. "That's what I'll do. I'll charge him with arson. He coulda burned the whole danged town down to the ground."

"Not hardly, dear," Jenny said. "Those are all adobe buildings along Calle Espejo. A fire only bakes the mud bricks harder than before. Now if he'd set fire to the plaza, he might have caused real damage to the town."

"He's not getting off scot free. He's a whiskey peddler. We don't cotton to anyone selling liquor, do we?"

"Why, no, dear, we don't." Jenny's wolfish grin chilled Frank to the bone. "Demon rum has ruined *so* many lives, after all."

"I could use a sip of that Taos Lightning Buck was selling," Frank mouthed.

"I'm sure you could use a lot more than that, Mr. Landry." Jenny made no effort to keep her voice down. She looked over her shoulder. A tall, man who looked as if he was carved from mahogany entered.

Frank caught his breath. Another lawman. This one wore a sheriff's badge. He was caught in the middle of a clutch of law dogs. Penned and at the mercy of the marshal's wife. All she had to do was tell what business they had tried to negotiate. Then he realized she couldn't do that without revealing her part in the illegal moonshine sales. And if she tried to accuse him of a crime, she also had to reveal her partnership with Buck Isaacson.

Jenny wouldn't do that because Frank decided her relationship with Buck was better described as a relationship— and one where they used that straw pallet with its blanket.

That thin sliver of hope kept Frank from blurting out something that would put a noose around his neck.

"Sheriff Thompson," Babson greeted. From his expression he'd just as soon have smallpox than share the same room with the other lawman. "What brings you by so late at night?"

"You know what," the sheriff growled. He stretched his long frame, took off his hat and slapped it against his thigh. A cloud of trail dust rose. The man's fingers had to be the longest and boniest Frank had never seen. He ran those fingers through thinning sandy hair, and then brushed small leaves from his full beard. Moving painfully, he sank into a chair.

"You look all tuckered out," Jenny said. She went behind the sheriff and began massaging his shoulders. The man closed his cold gray eyes and almost purred like a kitten.

"You do that divinely, my dear," he said.

Frank began to wonder about Jenny Babson. Even more, he wondered about her husband. Jasper Babson took no notice of how comfortable the sheriff was with his wife. This wasn't the first time she had worked the kinks out of his tense shoulder muscles, Frank guessed.

"You're after the robbers?" Jenny asked. "And all the gold they stole from the bank?"

"Nobody cares about the money," Thompson said. "Gunning down Jaime Ochoa was their big mistake."

"Why?" Frank called. "Why is killing a banker worse than killing a marshal?"

"He was going to be the next territorial governor," Thompson said. "With him setting his ass down in the Place of the Governors, I'd have been appointed federal marshal for the whole territory."

Frank held back any more questions. The robbery was none of his concern. Neither was Jaime Ochoa's death and what it meant to local politics. He had a more dangerous trail to ride with Jenny and her husband, the Taos marshal.

He began to reconsider his plan of getting involved in the illicit Taos Lightning trade, no matter how good the product was.

"I can't add anything to what you likely know," Babson said. "Taos is pretty quiet."

"The robbers hightailed it, that's why. They took the gold with them and left the dead bodies behind."

"You here to attend Marshal Nolan's funeral?"

Thompson snorted. Jenny began rubbing the sheriff's temples to soothe him. It wasn't working too well. Color rose into his suntanned, leathery cheeks.

"There are other funerals I want to attend. The man who killed Ochoa. My deputy's been scouring the high country. Three of them are dead. Looks like they killed each other, fighting over the loot."

"So if you wait long enough, all you need to do is run down the survivor? That makes sense, Sheriff."

"I want to catch the two that's left so I can put nooses around their filthy necks," Thompson snapped. "Can you loan me a couple of your deputies to build my posse? If we give the crooks too much of a head start, they'll be out of the territory and down in Mexico."

"I only got one deputy," Babson said. "If we go over to the White Elephant, we might convince a couple of them drunks to ride with you."

"That's better than nothing," Thompson said. He patted Jenny's hand, pulled it down and gave the palm a quick kiss. The way he looked over his shoulder at her spoke volumes. Jasper Babson missed all that as he plucked the key ring from a peg stuck in the wall and turned toward Frank. He bounced the ring until the keys clacked together, then made a point of fastening it to his belt.

Without a word he preceded Thompson from the office. The sheriff stood and silently stared at Jenny for a moment, then left, trailing the marshal. She sighed heavily and came over to the cell where Frank futilely rattled the heavy iron door.

"You can't get out that way. I watched the blacksmith build the cells. Rafe is very good at his job." She heaved a sigh and added, "He's very good at many things."

"You seem to get around," Frank said.

"Were you joshing Buck about how much 'shine you wanted to buy?"

Frank shook his head.

"Let's get down to business, then," Jenny said.

67

"It won't do me any good locked up in here. And your ... husband ... took the keys with him."

"Jasper thinks that'll keep somebody from wandering by, looking in and on the spur of the moment letting you out. Or you could sweet talk somebody into unlocking the cell door." Jenny's grin told him how lucky Sheriff Thompson was, and maybe Buck and who knew who else around town. Rafe the blacksmith had probably been paid with a lot more than a few dollars from the town coffers for his work in the jailhouse.

"The lock is mighty strong. I know. I checked it first thing."

"I'll just bet you checked out a lot of things," Jenny said, moving closer. She pressed her bosoms against the iron strips. "You should keep looking. There's no telling what treasure you can find ... in the right place."

She reached up and began unbuttoning her blouse.

Frank saw the sliver chain dangling around her neck and disappearing into the chasm between her breasts.

"Go on. Dig around a mite. Don't be too rough. I'm kinda sensitive there." She thrust out her chest a little more.

Frank wiggled his fingers between the iron strips and caught the chain. Tugging gently he lifted what weighed the necklace down. A large skeleton key looked as if it was a twin to the one Jasper Babson had used to lock the cell door.

"Rafe was mighty generous, wasn't he? I'd thank him, but I suspect you already have—and better than I ever could." Frank curled his fingers around, savoring the sleek, warm flesh. Then the key slid free.

"Oh, lookee there at what you found," Jenny said. She giggled like a schoolgirl. She bent forward so he could slip the chain over her head. Frank almost dropped it.

His dextrous fingers worked the key with its chain

through the cell door. It took a few seconds but he finally opened the cell door and stood outside, a free man.

"Do you always carry keys to jail cells?"

"Only when my husband insists on doing dumb things. He wasn't much shakes as a deputy. As a marshal he's no better. Now come along. There's no telling how long it'll take him and Sheriff Thompson to find out they can't recruit a solitary soul for the posse."

"Thompson sounded intent," Frank said. He rummaged through drawers and found his six-shooter. It slid back into his holster. "If he offers enough, he'll get a few men."

"His deputy's already rounded up anyone interested in the dollar a day and a shot of whiskey when they get back."

"You know all the lawmen in these parts?"

Jenny smirked. "Even the ones I'm not married to. Sheriff Thompson is the best of the lot. His deputy, Four-Finger Wilkinson, comes close but the man is a bit too fast on the draw, if you know what I mean."

Jenny Babson went to the door and chanced a quick look outside. She motioned for him to follow. Frank wasted no time. He untethered Barleycorn, helped Jenny swing up behind him and then settle down. Her arms circled his waist and moved a bit lower to hang on more than was comfortable.

"That's not the pommel, is it?" she asked. She laughed at his discomfort. "Keep on riding straight down this street."

They hurried through the cold night. For a few minutes he thought they were returning to the house where he'd burned out the door, but a different route took them north of town. She laid her cheek against his back. Her warmth made him forget about being locked up or who her husband was.

And as suddenly as a lightning bolt, she jerked away and pointed to the side of the road.

"Down there. A house." Jenny distanced herself from him.

By the time Frank spotted the house, the chilly wind had gusted between them, cooling his back and his spirit.

He saw right away why she wanted to put some distance between them. The dark figure at the side of the tumbledown shack stepped out. Starlight glinted off the rifle barrel.

"Good evening, Buck," Frank called. "You don't look any the worse for your quick escape."

"Why'd you bring him?"

"Because he's got money to buy your lousy moonshine, that's why. And you weren't shy about saving your own hide back in town. You could have let me get through the tunnel first."

"I knew it was your badge-toting husband outside. He wasn't going to do anything to you."

"If he ever caught wind of our business deal, he'd string me up alongside you and those two owlhoots you've got running the still."

Buck stepped closer and peered up at Frank. "You really have money or were you just pulling my leg?"

"I've got money," he assured the man. Buck's grip on the rifle was a bit too tense for Frank's liking. A misstatement now put someone in the ground.

"Tether your horse around back and come on in.

Jenny slid down and started to accompany Frank. Buck yanked her arm and they went into the shack. Their argument could be heard all the way to town. For a moment Frank considered abandoning his scheme to become a player in the game of moonshining. All he had to do was wheel around and gallop away. With any luck he could be halfway to Santa Fe by sunup and at a second sunrise lounging in the best hotel the territorial capital had to offer.

But he had worked through the numbers. For as little as five hundred dollars he could supply about every small town in northern New Mexico, and that included the military outposts from Fort Union to Fort Wingate. Six months and he'd have ten times his initial investment.

Sell out then and find something as profitable elsewhere. It was a sweet plan.

He glanced over his shoulder along the trail he and Jenny had ridden to get to the cabin. Safety. The argument in the cabin raged. Opportunity.

He secured Barleycorn to a hitch post and made sure his pistol rode easy in its holster before he went into the shack. Jenny sat on a rickety chair, arms crossed over her breasts and looking daggers at Buck. The moonshiner had leaned his rifle against the far wall and stood, hands thrust into his coat pockets, glaring back at her.

"Now that we've cleared the air," Frank said. "Let's get down to business."

"I don't know if we ought to keep runnin' the still much longer," Buck said. "There's lawmen swarmin' all around huntin' for the bank robbers. Killin' all them folks didn't do me any good, not the way it stirred up sentiment against any lawbreaker."

"The sheriff said a trio of them were dead," Frank said. "That leaves two out in the mountains somewhere. If anything, this is a good time to speed up your work. All the law dogs are out of your hair and chasing their own tails."

"More 'n the sheriff and his deputies are out there," Buck said.

"What do you mean?" Frank heard the anger in Buck's voice. He wanted to keep up a steady supply of corn liquor, but something was bothering him. And it wasn't only Sheriff Thompson and his posse poking around, hunting for the banker's killers.

"Strangers are ridin' through. I don't know if they're reporters or Pinkertons. Might be Pinks. I wouldn't put it past the governor to hire an entire company of them."

"She wasn't a Pinkerton," Jenny said sullenly. "Not from the *loving* way you described her."

"She wasn't here for her health. She had the look of someone on a mission."

"What are you going on about?" Frank demanded. The notion of riding away appealed to him more every second. Buck hadn't struck him as faint hearted before. He increasingly did.

"She wore a six-gun slung at her hip. She rode as good as any man," Buck said.

"And she was as pretty as a sunrise, you said," Jenny mocked. "Or was it that you wanted to wake up in the morning sunlight alongside her in bed?"

"Shut up," Frank snapped before Buck started the argument all over. "What did she look like?"

"Red hair. The reddest I ever did see. More like spun copper, maybe. And her eyes. We looked at each other. I don't know how to describe it. She was all soft and yielding—and yet I had the feeling in my gut that she'd cut me down and never bat an eye."

"Green eyes? Oval face? She was dressed for the trail but in clothing that looked like they'd been made just for her?"

"Yeah, like that."

Frank leaned against the wall and shook his head. While the mystery woman riding through Taos might be anyone, he doubted it."

"Emily," he said in a choked voice.

"Yes!" Buck perked up. "I heard the telegrapher call her that. She was sending a telegram to Denver and said her name. Emily O'Connor."

Frank felt as if he had stepped off a cliff and fell endlessly.

Emily. His ex-wife. His ex-wife was another of Allister Legende's recruits for the Society of Buckhorn and Bison.

7

Patches of snow crunched under the hooves of Emily O'Connor's horse. She pulled up her collar when a stiff, biting wind swept down from higher on the mountain. The road from Santa Fe had been easy enough until she reached Taos. She had never slowed as she passed through the town and worked her way to high country along increasingly bad roads. Worse than the fetlock-deep mud in places and frigid conditions, she felt as if someone dogged her steps and watched her every move.

Now and then she stopped and looked around. No one behind her. No one anywhere in the windswept country with towering ponderosa pines and white-barked aspens trying to grow their leaves back because of feeble hints of spring. If the weather was any indication, it'd be weeks yet before enough warmth blanketed the land for those aspens and oaks and maples to begin their yearly resurrection.

But for now the barren land and snowy patches showed nothing but emptiness amid the pines and firs. That did nothing to erase her feeling of being watched.

"Sheriff Thompson," she said softly. "Are you out there?"

A final look down her back trail failed to reveal any other rider.

It was absurd that the sheriff would track her. He had been in Santa Fe to raise a posse because of doubts about the new Taos marshal's competency. Emily had learned a long time ago to avoid getting between two men intent on fighting it out. That went double for lawmen. There was never a winner when jurisdictions were questioned and legalities went by the wayside. The death of Jaime Ochoa had set off a series of responses more violent than any mining disaster caused by careless blasting.

Worse, Emily had instructions from Allister Legende to find and bring to justice whoever had killed Jaime Ochoa. Her mission matched those of the Santa Fe sheriff and the new Taos marshal. If she stepped into the path of any of those juggernauts she'd be plowed under.

She wiped away tears from her watering eyes when she saw the crudely lettered sign: High Lonesome Ice Company. Her destination wasn't far now. And it came none too soon for her. The cold cut all the way into her bones and forced her to clamp her teeth together to keep from chattering uncontrollably.

"Giddyup," she said, putting her heels into her horse's flanks. The sorrel tried to shy away, but she kept it under control. Riding faster than was safe along the snowy road, she reached the icehouse within fifteen minutes. The huge warehouse where blocks of ice were produced loomed some distance from the small house. Smoke curled from the house's rock chimney. Someone was home. She hoped it meant the end of her search. She hardly felt her toes or fingers after the long ride from Taos.

A gunshot caused her horse to rear. She kept the sorrel under control as it curvetted. Twisting in the saddle, she wheeled about to face the lone figure holding a long-barreled shotgun trained on her.

"Go away. Stop bothering me. I don't know anything!"

"Beth? Elizabeth Randall! It's me, Emily O'Connor. Don't shoot." She paused long enough to be sure her horse didn't spook again. If the sorrel decided to race toward the woman, another load of buckshot might end both their lives.

"Emily? Is that really you? I can't see your face with that scarf wrapped around your head. What are you doing here? Oh, never mind. I know. I know." Beth lowered the shotgun. Tremors shook her shoulders as she bent forward. She began sobbing.

Emily approached cautiously. She looked down as her friend straightened and composed herself.

"Come on in. You can tie up your horse around back," Beth Randall said. "It doesn't mind being stabled with mules, does it? Some horses do. Some do." Her expression showed the intense, debilitating strain she was under. She turned and walked listlessly to her house.

Emily secured her horse in the crude stable and pulled off the heavy saddlebags. The four mules hardly stirred as she went about tending the sorrel. Being out of the wind suited her horse more than sharing quarters with the balky gray, lop-eared mules. When she finished, she took a deep breath and summoned up courage to deal with Beth.

She stopped just inside the front door and looked around. Beth had always been a meticulous housekeeper. It now looked as if a tornado had blown through. Emily dropped her saddlebags just inside the door and closed it against the cold. The warmth was immediate, in spite of the logs in the fireplace having burned down to embers. If anything the faint heat was almost painful as circulation returned to her cheeks and lips.

"Let me fix some coffee," Emily said. "You don't look as if you've eaten in a month."

Beth made a vague dismissive gesture and dropped into a straight-backed wood chair by the fireplace. She kept the shotgun across her lap and stroked it as if she held a furry animal.

Emily fixed the coffee and put a cup into a saucer on the table beside Beth's chair.

"Let me take that. It's all right." Gently, she pulled the shotgun from her friend's hands. Rather than put it across the room, she set it down where Beth could grab it if the mood moved her. Emily saw how the shotgun was like a child's security blanket to her.

"I know why you're here," Beth said in a dull voice. "I don't know why he did it."

"Pete?" Emily sank into a chair near the woman. Beth spoke so low she hardly heard her over the broken whine of the wind sneaking through cracks in the walls.

"Oh, I know why he robbed the bank. We're not doing so good here. Business has been slow. Real slow. It always is during the winter, but we'd have gotten through the hard time. We always had before and knew the slump in business was coming. Who wants ice when all they have to do is reach out the front door and break off an icicle?

"Summer's always good. People want lots of ice then. We even found markets nobody tried before. Did you know doctors can use ice to make cuts and bumps numb? They do. They really do." Beth sipped at her coffee. This revived her. Color returned to her cheeks and she became more animated and more focused. "He didn't have to get involved with those lowdown snakes, but he was feeling panicky about the business. He thought he was letting me down by not having piles of money."

"I was in Santa Fe," Emily said. "When I heard the sheriff

saying he wanted to get a posse together, I asked a lot of questions. He is sure Pete is one of the men who killed the Taos banker."

Beth looked at her sharply.

"I don't want to believe he had anything to do with that. He was desperate to keep the icehouse running until ..." She paused to take another sip of the strong coffee. "We have a big contract to fill. A week. Two. He should have waited to deliver the ice."

"Where?" Emily wanted to move her friend's thoughts away from her bank robber and killer husband. When she was more comfortable talking, then would be the time to find if she knew where her husband hid.

Emily felt guilty taking advantage of Beth this way, but Legende had sent specific orders. She had received the telegram in Santa Fe and replied that she was on her way to find the culprits. It was only after that she knew for sure that one of the men the Society wanted captured was the husband of her old friend.

She and Beth had met in Chicago so many years ago. Beth was the daughter of the owner of a huge slaughterhouse. That carried social ambiguity. Such a bloody profession brought huge floods of money. The part of society that accepted the money as their entrée looked down their snooty patrician noses at how the money was made. Similarly, those who celebrated butchering hogs were less likely to accept Beth and her family socially because of their immense wealth.

Emily had provided a bridge for Beth, giving her the cachet to enter high society, but all that had become moot when the Panic of '73 wiped out the family fortune. Her father had suffered a debilitating stroke and her mother had killed herself in disgrace. She and Beth had drifted apart, their paths crossing only briefly in Denver when Beth announced she was marrying Peter Randall.

The man hadn't been well off but had money enough to start the icehouse business. After that Emily had lost touch, only hearing about Beth and her entrepreneur husband occasionally. In a way she felt sorry for the poor woman. Beth lived with a dark cloud over her, almost all caused by family rather than anything she'd done. Even in the best of times, she never quite fit in anywhere. Hidden away up in the New Mexico mountains, making and shipping ice, seemed the best she could ever hope for.

"Why are you here, Emily?" Beth asked suddenly. "There's nothing you can do for me or Peter."

"Don't be too sure. You know me. I have connections in high places."

"You're saying I should tell my husband to turn himself in and you'll see that he gets a fair trial?"

"You make it sound as if that's impossible." Emily hated to admit it, but she thought that herself. She had heard the vitriol in Sheriff Thompson's tone. He wanted revenge. Reading Allister Legende's telegram gave her the same feeling. Jaime Ochoa had been a politically connected man. Whoever sent orders to Allister Legende had no reason to see that Peter Randall walked away a free man. Political schemes had been disrupted. The power structure had been inconvenienced by the bank president's death.

That might be worse than Thompson taking his friend and mentor's death personally.

"I know Peter had nothing to do with the killing, but ... but the robbery. He must have been there. For the past few weeks he's bemoaned our financial situation. The bank wouldn't lend us any money." She stared straight ahead as if hearing something in the distance. "We could have gotten the money after the delivery to Arizona."

"You ship ice all the way down into Arizona?"

"To Tombstone," Beth said. "Ice there is worth its weight

in gold. Ten times as much. High Lonesome Ice Company is the only other supplier to the big saloons. They have insulated vaults and one shipment can last them well into June." She smiled wanly. "Rich miners will pay about anything for a sliver of ice in their whiskey."

"You don't know where he is, do you?"

Beth shook her head. A tear ran down her cheek. She never bothered wiping it away.

"What are you going to do if your husband can't deliver the ice?"

"The company goes belly up. If only I could deliver, that'd prove the company was valuable and I could sell it."

"Do you have any hired hands? Pete wasn't going to make that drive by himself."

"Speed is the watchword. No, we have a worker to help make the ice. He was always the second driver Pete could depend on. Squinty Houseman is a decent enough man, but I'd never trust him to make the trip alone."

Emily saw the problem right away. If Houseman reached the market with the ice and got top price, he'd keep on riding and Beth would never see a red cent. Even the most honest man in the world had to feel the temptation building, mile by mile as he got closer to Tombstone with a valuable commodity.

"What's his given name?"

"Joseph. Joe. But no one calls him that because, well, if you see him you'll understand."

"Joe Houseman," Emily mouthed. The name meant nothing to her. While she hardly knew every crook and reprobate west of the Mississippi, she had accumulated quite a mental list of the most notorious. They had their uses, should she cross trails with them.

Beth suddenly jerked around, grabbed the shotgun and hefted it. She cried out and pulled the trigger. The hammer fell on a spent cartridge. She hadn't reloaded after firing into the air earlier to deter Emily.

"What is it?" Emily was on feet and had her derringer ready for action, having taken off her gun belt with its heavy six-shooter she had worn on the trail. She caught sight of a face at the window. "Wait here. And don't shoot me."

Beth sank back into the chair. Her color was gone again, and she trembled like an aspen leaf in a high wind.

Emily opened the door a crack and peered out. Then she yanked the door inward and burst out into the cold mountain air. The wind hit her like a slap in the face. She was instantly alert as she looked around. The sound of footsteps crunching in a patch of snow around the side of the house alerted her to the trespasser's location.

"Come out," she called. Then she whirled around, derringer ready. A moving figure at the rear of the house made her fire. The .45 caliber double-D kicked hard in her hand. She had a second barrel and waited for the fleeing figure to poke his head back. She'd not miss when he exposed his position again.

Cursing under her breath, she made her way to the rear and peeked around into the stable. Her sorrel tugged hard at the reins, trying to break free. She used the horse as a shield and dropped to her knees to look under the horse's belly. Again she got off a shot. And again she missed.

Emily fumbled to reload, then retraced her path to the front door, thinking the intruder intended to enter. She caught sight of him bent low as he ducked out of the stable and running toward the icehouse. Two more quick shots caused him to veer and take refuge in the huge structure.

Reloading her popper as she hurried, she knew the danger she faced. So far the man hadn't shot back. If he had a six-shooter she was completely outgunned.

"Quite skulking about," she called when she reached the

GUNSMOKE AND ICE

half-open door leading into the icehouse. Pumps for moving water, tanks and frames filled the warehouse. She paid no attention to the details. Finding the man and identifying him mattered more.

For a brief instant she worried that she pursued Pete Randall and that the man only wanted to see his wife. Emily finally got a quick look at the man when he moved between frames for holding ice blocks.

She caught her breath. The fleeting glimpse made her think she was chasing her ex-husband. A second look convinced her this wasn't so. This man had darker hair and no beard, though his bushy mustache and thick sideburns gave the impression of a beard. He certainly dressed as well as Frank Landry, but Frank would never wear such a gaudy beaded hatband or stick an eagle feather into it.

Moving quickly she followed the outer wall and once more caught sight of the man hunkered down behind a pump designed to lift water into a tank from a stream farther downhill. She drew a bead but held her fire. A stray bullet would damage important machinery. Beth didn't need the extra trouble and expense of fixing it.

Her hesitation gave the man the chance to dash for a side door. He slammed hard into it and knocked it off its hinges. Door and man crashed to the ground. By the time Emily reached the doorway, the man had used the door as a toboggan and sledded down a steep, snowy slope. She fired twice more but the distance was too great for the short-barreled hideout gun.

The man crashed into a pine tree, rolled and got to his feet. He shook his fist at her in futile rage and then disappeared into the trees.

Realizing she stood exposed if the man decided to return fire, she slipped back into the icehouse. The imposing equipment loomed above her. A cursory search revealed nothing to give her a clue as to the man's identity. It hadn't been Pete. She was sure of that.

"And it wasn't Frank," she said to herself. "Now why would I think he'd be up here?" Shaking her head at such a crazy notion, she returned to the house. She had some business to conduct with Elizabeth Randall.

8

Someone followed her.

No matter how hard she tried, Emily O'Connor wasn't able to catch a glimpse of whomever dogged her through the woods leading up to the icehouse. She reached the huge structure and rode around it, then urged her horse to a full gallop down the icy, muddy trail leading back to Taos. Her hope of flushing out the spy faded with every hoofbeat. By the time her horse was lathered and gasping for air, she gave up.

While no stranger to the wilderness, she preferred a smoke-filled room and a high-stakes poker game. On occasion, she even accepted a cigar offered by another player intent on taunting her. When she lit up and puffed away on the stogie with the best of them, she gained a small advantage. With the stakes she played for, that often meant walking away with a carpetbag full of greenbacks.

But she wasn't the trailsman so many in the Society of Buckhorn and Bison were.

"Especially Frank," she said, spitting out the words. Her

ex-husband frequented all the saloons in a town peddling his whiskey, but his sales calls often took him to obscure spots and towns that had popped up only weeks—days!—before. He had a special knack for finding boomtowns and exploiting them while they flourished and even as they declined.

She sat her horse listening and watching apprehensively. Her frenzied gallop had frightened the critters in the forest. As she let her sorrel recover its wind, those tiny scurry-scurry noises returned. A woodpecker hammering its way into a pine tree mining for tasty bugs. The small rustling sounds of rabbits and other small animals darting through the brush. The soft wind gusting about high in the conifers. And nothing of any human rider following her.

She worried that she was developing a paranoia fueled by Allister Legende. Forcing her to take on Society chores was alien to her way of living. Her hand drifted to a pocket in her split denim riding skirt and traced the outline of her derringer. For Society missions a six-gun was a better choice. This forest wasn't the drawing room or fancy gaming club she frequented. She considered returning to Beth's house and fetching the six-gun she had strapped on for the ride here from Taos. Its comforting weight at her hip kept trouble at a distance, but Emily wasn't as adroit with it as she was the derringer.

"Why me?" She heaved a sigh. She knew the reason Legende had sent her after Jaime Ochoa's killer. She was already in Santa Fe and therefore nearby to the source of the problem. More likely, all his other operatives were on other assignments. The tone of his telegram told her more than a bank president dying was at stake.

Revenge. Her orders weren't to bring in Ochoa's killers. She was to eliminate the man or men and leave their corpses for coyotes to fight over. Whoever pulled Allister Legende's strings had a master plan disrupted by the death. A loan that wouldn't go through now? A personal friend being murdered? Something else. Jaime Ochoa had been connected politically. He might have been groomed for more than mere governor of New Mexico Territory.

The assignments were often wrapped up in mystery with a distinct core of politics involved.

She doubted her orders now carried any different a motivation. Politics.

Walking her horse back up the steep trail tired it quickly. She wasn't as chipper as when she'd set out that morning, either. A talk with Beth and then a short nap seemed in order.

She rode to the house and tied up her horse at the side. She unslung her saddlebags and went to the kitchen door, intending to find something to eat before taking that nap. Emily froze when she heard a horse nickering. Dropping the saddlebags she turned slowly and looked around.

Just past the corner of the icehouse she caught sight of a horse's tail flicking back and forth. Then the horse disappeared. A quick glance over her shoulder told her Beth was inside, working in the kitchen. Her head drifted back and forth past the window. Emily even heard the woman singing softly to herself.

She reached into her skirt pocket and drew the derringer. Walking carefully to avoid making a sound to warn the intruder, she crossed the yard and went to the towering icehouse. She heard the horse putting up a mild protest now. She edged around the icehouse and saw that the horse, still saddled and a rifle thrust into a sheath, had been left alone. A door into the warehouse creaked mournfully as the mountain breeze moved it back and forth.

Emily went to the horse and patted its neck. The horse

was uncomfortable with her being so close, but she had no intention of riding it. She slid the Winchester from the saddle sheath and worked the lever. A fresh round slid into the chamber.

Feeling more confident with the rifle as well as her two-shot .45 popper, she poked open the door using the Winchester's barrel.

A gust of stale air blew out. She caught hints of sawdust and machine oil and something more.

"Peppermint," she said. "Peppermint scented hair tonic." The aroma was fresh. In the cold and wind along the mountain ridge, such a scent would have blown away if it had been left by Peter Randall. She doubted Beth or any self-respecting woman, would ever use such a pungent perfume. The fancy-dressed man she had run off before, though, was the kind who would delight in such a scent after a shave and a haircut.

Shadows cloaked the machinery inside the warehouse. She wasn't quite sure how everything worked, but water pumped from a lake just down the hill flowed into large vats. In each vat wooden dividers allowed ice the size and shape of a coffin to form when fans blew air across the surface. There was more to the machinery that she hadn't figured out. Chemicals beneath the vats blew increasingly chilled air to freeze from all directions. On the far side of the warehouse huge insulated rooms stored the manufactured ice.

She kicked her way through mounds of sawdust. Listening hard she tried to locate the intruder. A fan turned sluggishly overhead. The bearings needed greasing. Elsewhere a wind-driven pump chuff-chuff-chuffed to bring up water into a large overhead tank.

But no sound of anyone moving about. She might have been alone. Only she knew she wasn't. The horse outside hadn't come here on its own.

Emily worked her way past the equipment and into a loading area. A heavy wagon waited to be loaded. The sides were made of double panels and filled with sawdust for insulation. She stepped up and looked into the wagon bed. Compartments for a dozen or more huge blocks of ice stood empty.

A scraping sound made her look up. A man stood silhouetted on a catwalk high about a vat. He leaned far over the railing and peered into the vat. In this position he had his back to her. She lifted the rifle to her shoulder and sighted in on the middle of the dark shape.

"You come on down from up there of I'll fill you full of lead."

She hadn't expected the man to obey. She didn't expect the man to shoot at her, either. He whipped out a gun and triggered three quick rounds. They tore past her head with startling accuracy for such from the hip shooting and caused to her flinch. Emily's next round went wild because she fired as she ducked.

When she chanced a cautious peek around the wagon, the man was gone. Quick guesswork on her part eliminated directions he could go. She rushed to the rear of the wagon and peered out under it. Her guess was right. The man had found a ladder at the far end of the catwalk and scrambled down, taking two rungs at a time as he descended.

Resting the rifle against the wagon wheel to steady her aim, she fired when the man almost touched the floor at the bottom of the ladder. She had led him perfectly. Her round knocked him from the ladder.

She cursed when his body vanished behind a pile of sawdust. Some snipers claimed they had a feel for when they hit their target—and when they missed. She wasn't accustomed to firing a rifle, much less one she had stolen from a sneak thief, to have such confidence in herself. Moving forward, she jacked another round in and kept the rifle pointed straight ahead at the sawdust heap.

She got close enough to peer over it. Survival instincts took over. She dived forward into the sawdust just as a bullet sought her back. Emily winced as the hot lead creased her shoulder. With a puff of sawdust all around, she crashed down, then rolled.

More bullets kicked up tiny tornadoes in her wake. Scrambling for her life, she took refuge behind a pile of lumber used to make the forms for the ice.

"Give up. I promise not to shoot you." She waited to see if she coaxed a reply. All the gunfire and scooting about had caused her to lose track of where her adversary might have gone.

She cursed softly when he didn't answer. Her marksmanship wasn't good enough that she had ended his life, or even much wounded him. Stretching caused her own shoulder to throb. The length of the bloody crease along her right shoulder began to burn like fire.

Distracted, she almost missed where the man had fled. A tiny cascade of dirt and pebbles caused her to glance up. She fired wildly at the moving shape. Somehow the man had once more climbed onto the catwalk to gain the high ground advantage. Her first round tore splinters away just inches from his foot. Her second shot sailed past him. She saw a tiny spot of daylight appear in the roof. She had ventilated the warehouse's tin roof.

Return fire forced her to find shelter behind more substantial crates. After four rounds, the firing stopped.

She did quick calculations. The man must be out of ammunition. Even if he had a few spare shells in his gun belt, he had to be running low. And if he was one of the bank robbers, there was a chance he had exhausted all the rounds for his six-shooter. There wasn't much chance he had bought a box or two of ammo while on the run. If he'd had even a brief firefight with Sheriff Thompson's posse, he was that much closer to needing bullets.

Emily rushed to the ladder and began climbing. She made her way up to the catwalk slowly, trying to keep the rifle aimed above her should the man appear at the top of the ladder. She was almost to the last rung when she heard receding footfalls. He was running, not fighting.

Throwing caution to the wind, she popped up and balanced on the narrow walkway over the vats of freezing water. The ones immediately under her feet were completely frozen. A half dozen huge blocks were held by the wood frames. The next vat along the walkway had half-frozen water and the third one, the farthest, had a funnel above pouring in fresh water pumped from the overhead tank.

Tucking the rifle stock between upper arm and her body, she edged along the walkway. It swayed precariously as she moved. For a moment, she experienced a giddy sensation, then she found a safer way to advance. Rather than walking, she pushed her right foot out and drew up her left. Then she slid her right foot ahead again in a shuffling motion that kept the catwalk from swinging to and fro.

She clutched the rifle so hard her hand began to cramp. She took a second to swipe her palm across her skirt. In spite of the chilly air, she was sweating profusely.

"Give up. I've got you. All I want to do is find out why you've been following me."

Emily realized that earlier pursuit might have been nothing but her imagination. The mountains of New Mexico were strange to her and she wasn't much of a trailsman. This man skulking around the icehouse might have come in and knew nothing of her or Beth or—

The bullet almost took off her head. She jerked around involuntarily. Her arms flew up to regain her balance. She lost the rifle. Then she lost her footing. Screaming, she plunged downward.

For a moment, she thought she had hit a block of ice. Then the thin crust over the cold water cracked. She plunged downward into an ice water coffin.

9

Dandy Dan Dinkins fell flat on his belly and clutched his pistol so hard his hand began to shake. The approaching hoofbeats signalled that the sheriff had found his trail. Again. The man had to be part Apache to keep on a trail Dinkins had worked so hard to mask with dragged brush, long stints in half-frozen streams and eventually dangerous crossings of rocky patches so icy his horse stumbled constantly.

He sighted down the barrel of his Colt and waited. The rider came into view. It took all his willpower not to fire. He heard another horse some distance away—and it had to belong to another deputy. Dinkins let out a gust of air from his aching lungs when he could no longer hold his breath. His aim would have been off just because of his hammering heart.

Two more deputies joined the first for a palaver. They argued over where their quarry had gone.

Only snippets reached him, but he began to hope. The lead tracker had lost the tail and refused to admit it. He kept pointing downhill while the other two complained. None of them twigged to him being within gunshot.

He judged his chances of taking out all three law dogs when a fourth joined them. The three deputies were strangers to him. He knew Sheriff Thompson too well. The man was ferocious, tenacious and was rumored to take very few fugitives alive.

"Gustav is a better tracker than the lot of you," Thompson snapped. "If he says that away, we go that away."

One deputy said something too low for Dinkins to hear, but Sheriff Thompson reacted instantly. He backhanded the man so hard he tumbled from the saddle and crashed to the forest floor.

"What'd you go and do that for, Sheriff?" The deputy sat up and rubbed his cheek. Even at this distance Dinkins saw the red finger marks on the man's leathery cheek.

"I ain't some barroom cowboy. I get out from behind my desk more 'n I want to chase down killers like the ones we're after. You keep your opinions as to my competency to yourself. You hear me, boy?"

"I never meant anything by it, Sheriff. It's just that we're all sick and tired of wandering around and not finding squat."

"We found fresh horse apples back there," the scout said. "Somebody forked over a horse came this way within the past few hours."

"So where are they?" The deputy on the ground took a step back and held out his hands, palms forward, as if to push Thompson away. "I'm not complainin', Sheriff. Just asking."

"If you don't like the way I'm conducting this hunt, you hie on back to Taos."

"Do I get paid for the week I've been out here? You said two dollars a day and—"

"You don't get a red cent if you quit on me. Now what's it gonna be?" Thompson reared back and laid his hand on the butt of his holstered six-shooter. Dinkins hoped there'd be a shootout between the lawmen. One or more of them had to die in such an exchange, making it that much easier for him to get away.

"Downslope, I reckon," the deputy said, stepping up. He kept his distance from the lawman.

Dinkins heaved a sigh of relief when the small band of lawmen headed away from him. He had successfully hidden his trail this time, but Thompson wasn't giving up.

Neither was Dandy Dan Dinkins.

He had a double-crossing, no account, backstabbing former partner to find. When he found Pete Randall and the loot he had taken, he was going to plug him in the gut so he died real slow, bleeding inside to cause the most pain possible. Then, with the gold weighing down his horse, he was bound for Mexico, warm weather, smooth tequila and hot señoritas.

Dinkins made his way through the thicket and retrieved his horse. The tired animal resented being pulled away from a tuft of sere winter grass. In a few weeks spring would deliver more grass than any horse could want. Now it was slim pickin's.

He walked his horse uphill, heading back to the icehouse. Randall had made a beeline for the place, and Dinkins wanted to find out why. After a long hike, he saw the huge warehouse looming above treetops and caught the pungent ammonia odor that permeated the whole area. The chemical made his nose drip and sent tiny daggers up into his head.

He looked around but saw no one near the house across the yard. He went to the house and peered inside through a dirty window, ducking when the woman inside spotted him. He had to hide—fast. He trotted across the yard and used the warehouse to hide, then ducked into the huge structure. The darkness blinded him for a moment. When his eyes adjusted, he climbed a ladder and edged along a rickety catwalk. Vats filled with water in various stages of freezing stretched below him like ice floes in the Arctic.

"About the size of a coffin," he muttered. Squinting, he tried to make out if any of the blocks of ice were anything more. Randall had a reason for returning here. If it hadn't been for the posse, Dinkins would have run him to ground. The ice blocks might make a safe place to stash the loot from the bank robbery.

No need to dig a hole that might be found with so many lawmen on his trail. Randall had been shot up pretty bad. He wasn't going to run far in his condition.

Dinkins began a more careful look into the wood-framed blocks of ice. Ammonia pumped along beneath them and fans carried fresh air across the surface. Somehow the chemical froze the water faster than the frigid mountain temperatures did. Fresh water pumped from a lake lower down the hillside furnished the basic product to be frozen. It was stored in a leaky overhead tank that caused him to duck and dodge the artificial rain.

Dinkins reacted like a stepped on mountain rattler and then froze when a voice called out, "You come on down from up there or I'll fill you full of lead." He slapped leather, drew and fired at the source of the command below him on the warehouse floor, in the direction of a large covered wagon.

His first shot missed. He fanned off two more.

Rather than stand still and present a target any eight-year-old boy could hit with a squirrel gun, he bent low and hurried along the catwalk, hunting for a way to the warehouse floor where he wouldn't be a sitting duck. The ladder he had used to get to the catwalk was the nearest way down. He landed hard at the base, skipping two or three rungs with every step in his descent. Another round tore into the rung just above his head.

"Give up. I promise not to shoot you."

He tried not to laugh out loud. Whoever fired at him, and it sounded like a woman's voice calling out stupid orders, had ambushed him. It was only luck that her first round had missed. Believing anything such a back shooter said was a good way to end up worm food.

Dinkins reached the warehouse floor and got off a couple more shots, driving his attacker behind a pile of lumber. From this angle she could wait him out. He had no idea if others back at the house would come rushing over to join the fight. With some reluctance, Dinkins climbed the ladder again to gain the advantage of high ground.

He fired at her, driving her away to find refuge behind crates. Atop the ladder, he had only one escape route. Moving as fast as possible and carefully enough not to cause the catwalk to collapse, he made his way the length of the warehouse. A second ladder down at the far end gave him a way out.

Dinkins turned and stepped down, foot on the top rung.

"Give up. I've got you. All I want to do is find out why you've been following me."

He looked up, startled. She had climbed the other ladder and risked the precarious catwalk to come after him. Dinkins took careful aim and fired. The woman let out a cry, wobbled for an instant, then toppled into the vat below. He heard her body land hard on ice. Creaking and cracking followed by a splash assured him she was a goner. She had tumbled into one of the ice coffins.

Leaning over the railing, he saw that she had broken through the thin, freezing cold crust and sank entirely underwater now. If she didn't drown, she'd freeze. That was good enough. She was a goner, and he didn't have to waste another of his rapidly diminishing bullets on her. He scooped up the rifle she had dropped, surprised to see she had used his own rifle in her ambush.

Dinkins made a final sweep of the vats, wondering if Randall had hidden the gold in one of the blocks of ice. Then a loud call from the door leading into the warehouse sent him running. Whoever was in the house might have a small army backing them up. There hadn't been time to scout out that possibility. He grabbed the sides of the ladder and kicked out. He didn't bother stepping down rung by rung. Instead he slid to the floor using the sides of the ladder as railroad tracks.

Wasting no time, Dinkins stepped outside and looked around. There hadn't been a trace of his double-crossing partner inside. The blood trail down the mountainside was still his only hope of tracking Randall and making him tell what he'd done with the loot.

But the sheriff had a posse, maybe more than one, scouring the hillside. Dinkins ran the risk of not finding Randall first, but running afoul of the law was a bigger concern. As he retrieved his horse, sheathed his rifle and rode away slowly, making as little noise as possible, a plan built in his head, layer by layer.

The sheriff and his deputies had no idea who they chased. If they found two bodies, how would they know they weren't the bank robbers they hunted?

"So I need a couple bodies. Fat chance." He looked down at his tattered clothing. This was the best way to identify him as a robber. Better to run Randall to ground and then hightail it out of the territory.

He found a road and followed it around the mountainside. From the pipes and equipment along the road, it led to the lake where the icehouse pumped water. He got his bearings, decided the last spot where he had seen traces of blood wasn't far off and rode toward the lake. It was all he had.

Less than ten minutes on the road, he heard voices from a thicket. He caught his breath. Two men. At least. Randall would be alone. The chances were good he had come across a small band separated from the sheriff's posse.

He saw a pile of brush that couldn't possibly grow up over

the head of a mounted man. A quick check of the ground showed a clumsy attempt to hide a trail. The law dogs had no reason to conceal themselves like this. Moreover, the tracks were cut into soft earth, then frozen, showing they'd been made some time earlier before the ground had frozen.

He rode around the brush and saw it had been heaped up to conceal a well-traveled road. Somebody wanted to hide this track through the woods, probably from the law.

Dinkins took a deep breath. His head spun. Not only did he catch the scent of a wood fire, something more powerful mingled with the smoke.

He grinned. "Moonshine." His mouth watered, thinking of the potent taste burning in his mouth and pioneering a fiery path all the way down to his belly. He had blundered across a still making Taos Lightning. More than once he had sampled the liquid fire from a clay jug. It had turned him every which way but loose.

Moving parallel to the hidden road, Dinkins finally came on the still. Two men stood outside a tumbledown shack, lost in deep conversation. He shielded his eyes from the early spring sun and tried to get a better look. A slow smile crept to his lips.

If he wanted two bodies to decoy the sheriff and his posse, these two were perfect. The one waving his arms around like a windmill in a high wind was close enough in build and height to pass for Pete Randall. The other man, better dressed and more composed, was a dead ringer if Dinkins dressed him in his own trail-worn clothing.

There was an added bonus in getting rid of his duds. The second man wasn't gussied up in finery Dandy Dan Dinkins would choose, but he wasn't shabbily dressed, either. Replacing rags with those tailored garments would go a ways toward boosting his self confidence. He frowned, though, thinking how to avoid putting a bullet hole or two in the other's coat and vest. Bloodstains might pose a problem, too.

Dinkins shrugged it off. If necessary, dirt smeared across any hole or blood splotch headed off any unwanted questions should anyone even notice or care.

The attitude of the two arguing men showed they thought they were alone. The moonshiner had chosen this spot to be hard to find so the law wouldn't bust up his livelihood. Another bonus would be sampling a bottle or two of the 'shine after he killed the pair.

Always one for the straightforward approach, Dinkins drew his six-gun and rested it across the saddle in front of him. It did little to hide it from the men, but they wouldn't have much time to react. He rode forward, not trying to keep his attack a secret.

The one he pegged as the moonshiner let out a warning cry and grabbed for a shotgun leaning against the shack's wall. Dinkins took him out first. The bullet caught the man in the temple. The moonshiner reached for the shotgun and kept reaching. His dead body slammed into the wall. Slowly flowing down against the splintery planks as if he melted, he ended up on his face in the dirt. His lifeless fingers were inches from getting to his greener.

Dinkins turned to the better dressed man, only to find he had killed the wrong one first. The man's long blond hair swung around his shoulders as he moved with easy, coordinated effort to throw down. His mustache twitched as a sneer curled his upper lip. And he drew back his fancy coat to show a six-shooter in a cross-draw holster. Dinkins had never seen men draw from such a rig faster. More than one gambler with that style of holster had died thinking he was faster than Dinkins.

The first round cut through the brim of Dinkins' hat and sent it flying. The second shot came a fraction of a second before the robber regained his senses. If he had instinctively tried to grab his flying hat, that follow-up round would have drilled him squarely in the head.

From the tiny pop! the six-shooter he faced wasn't a large caliber. He ignored that. A man died as surely with a .22 in his head as from a .45.

Dinkins bent low and fired under his horse's neck. But his target was gone. Not only was the duded-up gun slick fast on the draw, he understood the danger.

Dinkins had harvested one body for his scheme. He needed the other because the adroit gunman was a perfect match physically. More than that, Dinkins wanted the man's clothing. He was richly dressed for anyone in New Mexico.

"I got it wrong. You're not the one I want," Dinkins called. "I done shot him, and that was a damned mistake. I apologize for being so quick on the trigger. Come on back. Let's talk this out over some 'shine like the gentlemen we are."

His adversary didn't respond. Dinkins had hoped for was an angry retort so he could locate him. He kicked free of his horse and took shelter behind the shack. All he heard was water boiling and moonshine dripping into a tin washtub. A quick look around the side of the building disappointed him. His victim was nowhere to be seen.

Dinkins slipped through the door into the shack. The mere odor of the potent 'shine came close to making him knee-walking drunk. It was that powerful. He dipped a tin cup into the tub and sampled. If the aroma was knock-down strong, the actual popskull was ten times worse. He started to take another sip, then heard a horse thundering away.

He cursed, hesitated, then downed the liquor. It stiffened him from the toes all the way to the top of his head. He ducked out of the shack, glanced to be sure the moonshiner was dead, dead, dead. Then he mounted his horse and lit out after his fleeing quarry.

Catching the man was even more important now. Not only did he want the man's corpse, he couldn't let him warn other moonshiners of a killer loose in the mountains. Dodging the sheriff and his posse was bad enough. Having frightened moonshiners taking aim at him added to the problem of finding Pete Randall. They knew every hidden trail in the hills and stood a better chance of ambushing him than the sheriff did of tracking him down.

Dinkins found the fleeing man's trail without any trouble. He rode hellbent for leather through the forest. Galloping along the other man's trail turned more dangerous. He reached a road. From what Dinkins remembered of the terrain, the road led to the lake. And if he took it the other direction, it went back to Taos.

He came to a quick decision since the road was such a jumble of hoofprints and wagon tracks in the mud caused by half melted snow and ice. Without any way to determine which direction his quarry had ridden, he went toward the lake. The man he sought had been dealing with a moonshiner. That meant he had no interest in cozying up to the law.

The only decision Dinkins had to make now was what to do if he didn't find him. He had one body. Would that be enough to decoy the posse? He doubted it.

And he wanted that change of clothes. It was downright embarrassing wearing the tatters he now sported.

10

Emily O'Connor tumbled off the catwalk. For an instant she thought she could take flight like a bird and flutter off. Then gravity wrapped its powerful fingers around her. She plunged downward. At the last instant, she twisted around and landed flat on her back.

The entire length of her spine was chilled by ice. She had landed hard in the vat and flopped about on top of the block. She tried to sit up. The ice under her creaked and groaned, then broke. She dropped only a few inches, but that was enough to take her breath away.

Emily opened her eyes and saw the world above her in frigid blue ripples. Then she tried to breathe. Only ice water entered her nose and mouth. The world began to fade. Fast.

The next thing she remembered was being shaken hard. Ice crystals cascaded from her like glass shards. Her eyelids were frozen shut. Rubbing her eyes with a cold hand did little to bring her back to full consciousness, but a distant voice did.

"Come on, Emily. We've got to get you to the house. Fire.

Warm you up. You'll freeze to death if we don't take off those soaked clothes."

Beth! She tried to call to her friend, but her lips were blue and swollen. An arm circled her shoulders and lifted. She tumbled over the wooden side of the vat and lay facedown for a moment. The harsh ammonia from the machinery brought her around with a violent start.

"Smelling salts," she got out.

"That's what it is. That and what's used to freeze ice fast."

Bent double, she let Beth guide her from the vat through a slot where a couple boards hadn't been secured. Trying to walk proved hard. She stumbled forward and landed in sawdust. The urge to curl up and not move any more came almost overcame her. But in the back of her mind a voice said this was what it felt like to freeze to death.

Skinning her knees, she got to her feet clumsily. With Beth's help they crossed the yard and went into the house. Emily recoiled at the blast of heat from the iron stove. Before the cabin had seemed a tad chilly but comfortable enough. Now she felt as if she was burning up.

"Set yourself down by the stove. Not too close. I'll get some coffee. That'll warm your innards while the fire takes care of your outsides."

As her friend went to fetch the coffee, Emily rubbed her arms and tried to curl into herself for warmth. Edging closer to the radiant iron stove served her better.

"Take off that coat. Put this blanket around your shoulders. It's the warmest one I have. We traded a Navajo for it. Two Grey Hills."

Emily pulled it around her. Beth was right. The blanket trapped her body heat well. With shaky hands she picked up the coffee cup. Cradling it in both hands warmed her almost as much as taking a sip. It was black and bitter and exactly what she needed to speed her revival.

Before she had thought she was going to die. Now living was within her grasp—her grasp and the hot coffee cup.

"Who were you chasing?" Beth asked. "I saw a man on the catwalk, but I didn't get a good look at him." She sniffed loudly. "I certainly did not get a clean shot at the varmint. Did he push you into the ice machine?"

Emily nodded. Her strength came back.

"It's too late to chase him down. Maybe he's one of the bank robbers Sheriff Thompson is after."

"All the more reason to plug him," Beth said. "Go on. Get out of the rest of those wet things. I've got a robe you can wear until everything's dry."

Emily slowly stripped under the blanket. Switching to the robe exposed bare skin briefly, but she had regained her strength and agility now. Wearing the robe next to her skin with the Navajo blanket wrapping her gave the stove a chance to work its magic. In a few minutes she recovered.

"Doesn't look like frostbite," Beth said, examining her fingers. She touched Emily's lips. "Nope, not a bit of it. You were lucky I came along. Another minute and you'd have been a goner."

"I'd have drowned before I froze."

"That's likely." Beth refilled her coffee cup and settled down near the stove. "I can't tell if you're bringing all the trouble or if Pete's responsible. Things were hard before but not deadly dangerous like after you got here."

"Think of the robbery as a keg of blasting powder. Pete lit the fuse." Emily considered telling her savior about the Society of Buckhorn and Bison and how Allister Legende had sent her to bring the bank president's killers to justice.

Explaining about the Society and how she was involved was more than she wanted to tackle. Truth to tell, she wasn't up to getting into the politics of the killing. Jaime Ochoa had been slated for a bigger political role, and now he was dead.

That scuttled the plans of whomever sent Legende his orders. New Mexico Territory was a vast, wide-open range. The Spanish had ruled it for centuries and most of the land was pledged in land grants signed by the King of Spain.

Minerals and rangeland were extensive enough to make a man on the right side of the governor filthy rich.

"Pete always tried to do the right thing. It was, well," Beth fought for the words, "he never quite got it right. It was just the way he was. He meant well but failed to make it count for anything."

"I know men like that," Emily said. "In a two horse race always bet against them."

Beth smiled weakly and nodded.

"You haven't seen him?"

Beth looked up, her eyes hard. "You'll turn him in to the law. I hear it in your voice. I need him. I need him to keep the business running. We've got one last chance, and I won't do anything to jeopardize it."

"One last chance? The money from the robbery?" Emily frowned.

"No!" Beth shot to her feet and began pacing back and forth in front of the cast iron stove. Emily wished she could move. A cold breeze blew across her every time Beth blocked the heat.

"What do you mean? The money would keep the icehouse in business."

"I never knew Pete intended any such craziness. No, I mean we have that big contract to fill over in Arizona. It's likely our last, no matter how good we do financially, though."

Emily settled down and sipped at her coffee. She felt alive again. The last of the chilblains was gone, and fingers and toes wiggled just fine.

"The ice shipments to Tombstone have always been where our yearly profit was. Selling closer to home in New

Mexico was breaking even, but never did we make a decent profit. A living, barely, but never a sale to let us live it up."

"Something's happened to the Tombstone market?"

"There've been rumors of at least one ice company starting up there. Ice caves to the west of the town might supply some, but companies with equipment like ours see Tombstone as a big market."

"Building an icehouse in town cuts down on the long haulage," Emily said, nodding in understanding. "That reduces the price to tavern owners."

"Several of them are chipping in to run their own ice plant," Beth said. "They ought to have it going before summer. Until then me and Pete's ice will be all they have, as usual."

"Without Pete to drive, how are you getting the ice to Arizona?"

"Pete and our hired hand were supposed to set out any day now. I can't ask Squinty to make the trip alone."

"Squinty?'

"His name's Joe Houseman but you can guess how he got his moniker." Beth closed her right eye and peered at Emily making her laugh. "Just don't snicker when you see him. He's real touchy about it."

"But he calls himself Squinty?" Emily heaved a sigh. She saw reason beyond how dangerous it would be for a single driver to take the ice to market down south.

The odds were against Beth if she let her hired man make the trip alone.

She knew about temptation and being able to steal without any possibility of punishment.

"You're thinking about driving down with Squinty, aren't you?" Emily read the answer on Beth's face. "That's downright dangerous."

"The quicker we go, the quicker we get to Tombstone," Beth said.

A new card was dealt into Emily's hand, and this one showed even more danger. Having Squinty steal the money from the ice sales was one thing. The trail to Arizona was long and lonely. If Squinty had deeper, darker urges Beth would never arrive in Tombstone alive.

Allister Legende had entrusted her with running Pete Randall and the rest of his thieving gang to ground. Political undercurrents rippled all the way to Washington. She owed Legende for a great deal and felt a loyalty to him and the Society. Becoming a member in good standing had been her choice. At any time she could have walked away, but it served her, not only through financial support but camaraderie. The Society fulfilled her need to accomplish good deeds that benefitted more than her own passing desires.

So far, the assignments she'd been given had all ended satisfactorily. Even working with her ex-husband on occasion hadn't dimmed the shine on those accomplishments.

Legende had tasked her with bringing Jaime Ochoa's killer to justice. She had accepted. To walk away would be a betrayal of her honor and friendship.

Emily looked at Beth, forlorn and on the edge of exhaustion. Her husband had tried to save their business and made spectacularly bad choices. Beth had one last chance because Emily was sure that Sheriff Thompson and his posse would never stop until they caught Pete.

"I'll ride with you." Emily shook her head and looked around, wondering who had spoken. Then she realized she had. The decision forced her to turn her back on Legende in favor of another friend who needed her more.

"What do you mean? You want to accompany Squinty and me?"

"All the way to your Arizona buyers," Emily said. Her voice firmed. She became more confident and certain of her decision. "When do we leave?"

11

"I've got the market. All I need is the supply. You can expand your output, can't you?" Frank Landry looked at the still. While he needed to find places to sell the illicit moonshine distilled here, he wasn't sure how much more could be produced with this equipment.

"Well, now," Buck Isaacson said. "It's like this. I got other stills. More 'n just this one. I got a veritable 'shine empire workin' for me scattered all around these hills, as Jenny says all the time. You tell me what you need and see if I don't deliver."

Frank's brain threatened to blow up as he worked over all the possibilities. With the saloon owners he knew from selling them bonded whiskey, complete with the tax stamps, he had contacts throughout the territory. Even up in Colorado, if he wanted to smuggle the potent liquor over the mountains. That posed some problems. Raton Pass was tied up tighter than a banker's purse strings. Anything not rattling through on a train had to pass a toll gate. Buying off the man and his trigger-happy family running the toll road might prove too expensive. Other ways north existed, but those passes were higher and more dangerous, not only from nature but from roving bands of Indians.

"I think it's time we talked turkey. How much of a discount can I get for, say, fifty gallons."

"Fifty?" Buck blinked. He leaned his shotgun against the shed wall and scratched his chin. "That's more 'n I was fixin' to brew. But it's not out of the question. Not if you pony up some greenbacks in advance for me to buy the fixin's."

"A quarter to get going," Frank said. "And I'll see about supplying the jugs." He wanted all his moonshine to have a uniform look. One saloon barkeep showing it to the customers built a demand when the thirsty drunk drifted to another drinking emporium. He had seen this work with his legitimate whiskey.

It'd work for him with his illegal brand.

"Brand," he muttered. He'd have to think up something to call the moonshine.

"What's that?" Buck turned away from him.

"Nothing, I was just thinking out loud."

"He's not with you?" Buck made a grab for the shotgun.

Frm recoiled. Everything happened at once. Buck's fingers stretched toward his shotgun the same instant a bullet tore past Frank's ear and collided with the moonshiner's head. Frank stumbled away and turned toward the rider galloping toward the still.

He got a quick look at the rider before he hit the ground and rolled away to avoid the barrage coming his way. Frank got a quick look at the prone moonshiner. A shallow wound alongside Buck's head oozed blood. He wasn't sure how badly hurt the man was from a quick look. Head wounds always seemed worse than they usually were. But Buck lay unmoving.

Frank rolled over and over to avoid tiny puffs all around him. Every tiny tornado was a bullet seeking his flesh. He came to his knees, whipped out his Colt Navy and began firing.

His return fire forced the attacker galloping toward him to veer away and put distance between them. Frank worried this was a rival moonshiner. Starting a war between the various factions scattered throughout the Sangre de Cristos only complicated his business ambitions. Better to pay off a half dozen 'shiners than to have one disgruntled mountain man shooting up his rivals' stills.

Frank called out, hoping to strike a truce. His words vanished in the repeated reports from his attacker's six-shooter. Gunsmoke clouded the killer's aim, giving Frank a chance to duck and run for his horse. With a single bound, he set astride Barleycorn and galloped away into the surrounding forest.

He slowed quickly, cut off the trail he'd taken and made his way through the dense forest. Pine, spruce and Douglas fir clogged every route he took, but the pine needles on the forest floor effectively masked his trail. It took quite a bit of pressure to crush a fallen pine needle. A decent tracker would have no trouble, but it ate up time dropping down and closely studying the ground to find the fragrant, broken needles.

Behind him he heard the cursing ambusher coming for him. The man shouted out futile words of wanting to parley. After the unprovoked attack at the still, such jawing wasn't going to happen.

Frank reloaded his Colt Navy and made a wide circuit, taking care to move as silently as possible and leave no trail. When he came to the river used by the moonshiner, he splashed a few yards back toward the still, then left the watery highway. What he gained in hiding his trail, he lost in the sounds of sloshing about.

He made his way directly for the still. After surveying the area for a full minute, he acted. If they'd been attacked by another moonshiner, he'd be back when he gave up his hunt for a trail. Frank intended to be long gone by then.

He dropped to the ground and knelt beside the fallen owner of the still. While blood had caked on Buck Isaacson's temple, tiny spurts showed his heart still pumped. Frank shook the man gently and called his name.

"Wha? Jenny? Time to get up? Didn't hear no rooster."

"We have to leave, Buck. Right now." Frank helped him sit up. The man's eyes crossed, then focused.

"The consarned bushwhacker opened up on us without so much as a fare-thee-well."

"That's the way I saw it, too." Frank slipped his arm around the man's shoulders and pulled him to unsteady feet. "Did you recognize him?"

"Ain't never laid eyes on him before." Buck tried to pull away. "Got to defend my claim." He reached for the shotgun. Frank grabbed it first.

"I'll hang onto this for you. Let's mount up and get out of here. You're in no shape to fight over your still."

"You still want fifty gallons?"

Frank assured him that he did. This motivated Buck to walk a tad faster, if not more steadily. It took several tries to get him into the saddle. For a moment, Frank wasn't sure what to do with the shotgun. Then he handed it up. They needed all the firepower they could muster. He hoped Buck's head had cleared enough to know who the bad guy was if shooting started.

A quick assessment of where they were and the direction of Taos set Frank off through the woods. Buck followed without making any complaint, so Frank pressed on. Within ten minutes they came across a well-travelled road.

"Thataway," Buck said, pointing. The effort almost did him in. He slumped forward and came close to falling. Only Frank's quick grab held him on his horse.

The ride to Taos dragged into eternity. Frank was never happier to be at the end of a trip than when Buck pointed out an adobe house. Where they had met first was a hovel. This was hardly better, but had a lived-in look to it that made it more appealing. Barely had they halted than Jenny boiled out, looking all flustered.

"What have you got yourself into now, Buck Isaacson?"

"We were ambushed," Frank said, but he talked to the woman's back. She grabbed Buck around the shoulders and backed away from his horse. He fell heavily. Frank was impressed with how well she clung to the close to dead weight. If he had been pulling Buck down, he was sure they'd both have ended up in the dust. As it was, Jenny spun Buck around and had him inside by the time Frank tied their horses around back.

The cool, dark interior wrapped him up like a shroud. He hadn't been hit by any of the flying lead, but the entire adventure had drained him of his vim and vigor. Frank dropped into a chair and poured himself a little moonshine from a jug. The Taos Lightning kicked at his gut like a mule, but it brought him back to full alertness.

Jenny cooed over Buck and mopped away at the dried blood on his forehead.

"You'll be just fine, my darling. Just fine and dandy."

Buck kissed her hand and whispered something that made the woman giggle. Frank was glad not to have heard it. A second finger of the moonshine served him better.

Jenny left Buck in the bed and seated herself across from Frank. Her cold eyes pinned him like an arrow through the heart.

"What'd you get him into out there? Not another of them stupid moonshine wars? The last one cost ten good men their lives and left as many widows and grievin' girlfriends behind."

Frank explained the best he could.

"So you're sayin' you don't know who jumped Buck and you?"

"That's the Gospel truth," Frank said. He eyed the jug. Two drinks had made him a little woozy. A third might put him out like a light. He was considering it none the same when hoofbeats coming from the direction of the middle of town alerted him to trouble.

Jenny sat bolt upright. Her eyes went wide with fear.

"You get Buck on outta here. Both of you skedaddle." She reached across the table and yanked at his sleeve.

"Roll him under the bed. There's no way we can both get out of here. He's passed out," Frank said.

"Go, go, I'll think of somethin' to tell him."

He didn't need to ask who Jenny meant.

Frank dropped down into the hollow around the indoor well and clung to the pump handle as the marshal bulled his way in. He peered over the low wall and watched the expression on Jasper Babson's face go from fierce to confused.

"What are you doing here, Jenny?" The marshal waved his six-gun around and finally trained it on the unconscious Buck.

"I might ask the same of you," she snapped. "I got the call that a man'd been shot, so I came over to tend him. A good thing, too. Buck'd have up and died if I hadn't tended him."

"He's a moonshiner," Marshal Babson declared.

"He's a hero. He ought to have a medal pinned on his chest," she insisted.

Frank caught his breath. He knew where this was heading and didn't like it one little bit.

Jenny pushed the pistol away so her husband wouldn't kill Buck in the bed.

"He saved me from that fancy dressed fellow."

"The whiskey peddler?"

"He's the one. He tried to force his attentions on me. They were unwanted attentions, I might add." Jenny crossed her arms and stood so that she blocked her husband's view of the kitchen and the well.

Frank might end up being the most hunted man in New Mexico Territory, but the woman gave him a slender chance to escape. He edged toward the back of the well area where a drainage hole had been drilled through the thick adobe. It was small but it was mostly clogged with mud. Frank began digging as quickly—and silently—as he could.

"Are you hurt?"

"You get those filthy hands off me, Jasper Babson. You've been haulin' dead critters out of the street and never bothered to apply any soap to your hide. You know what I think about you having dirty paws and smelling like a slaughterhouse."

"Did he do it here?"

"Who?" she asked. "Oh, *him*. Yes, my darling. This very spot," Jenny declared. "Why, he got himself all likkered up on that horrible devil's brew to become man enough. That's a jug of it on the table and that's the very glass he swilled it from." She shuddered delicately, turned her face away and stared hard at Frank pawing through the mud. She mouthed something for his eyes only.

He didn't have to read her lips to know what she said. He was hurrying as fast as he could.

"There's still a drop of two in the bottle." Babson moved the glass and jug around on the table.

"He had to get his courage up for what he intended doin' to me, Jasper. He tried to force me to drink some, but I wouldn't have none of it. No, sir, not a bit of that devilish elixir."

"Why's Buck there a hero? You said he saved you?" With some reluctance, Jasper Babson pushed the glass with its remaining drop of mountain dew across the table.

"He did. It was a terrible fight. They traded blows like it

was some kind of bare-knuckles world championship match. When the peddler saw he was gettin' whupped good and proper, he shot Buck. And I been tryin' to keep him from dyin' to thank him for being such a gentleman defendin' my sacred honor."

"Your honor?" Babson sounded skeptical.

"Why, yes, Jasper, my sacred honor. Since you were out catchin' crooks and keepin' the peace in town, it was good to have someone defend my purity."

Frank almost laughed when he heard that. Then he dug faster. The drainage hole opened up enough for him to twist around and shoved his shoulders through. He got tangled up a mite, then popped out and fell into a half-frozen puddle.

The sounds inside the house told him the marshal was inspecting his wife for any signs of violation. That might take a spell. He hoped it would. He caught up Barleycorn's reins and led the horse away as he scraped off mud from his clothing. A complete change was necessary, but first he had to hightail it out of Taos.

Not only did he have some unknown gunman trying to fill him full of lead, he'd have the Taos marshal after him for a crime he never committed. That wasn't anything unusual, but he wished he had been able to talk with Buck a few minutes longer.

Even his dream of setting up a moonshine empire in New Mexico was shattered.

"Giddyup, Barleycorn. We need to head for the high county. Pronto."

The gelding snorted in contempt, then lengthened its stride. In spite of Frank Landry's ways, breaking in a new owner would be too hard.

12

Emily O'Connor completed her patrol around perimeter of the High Lonesome Ice Company property and found nothing. That worried her as much as if she had found a dozen bank robbers hiding in the stable or a Ute war party ready to attack. She felt she missed some small trace. This wasn't her world, not fighting off stalkers or men sneaking a look from behind trees.

Even a small trace that someone was out there would have soothed her ruffled feathers. As it was, the emptiness around the icehouse taunted her. What had she missed?

"He'll be here soon."

Emily jerked around at Beth's words. She tried not to lift the six-shooter in response and almost succeeded.

"You're mighty jumpy. What did you find?" The concern Beth showed fed her own uneasiness, and it was all her doing.

"Nothing," Emily said. "Where's your hired hand been?"

"He lives in Taos and only comes out when there's work to be done. The icehouse doesn't take much work and ... and Pete was able to do most of the repair work. Together we kept up pretty well without Squinty doing much more than helping to move heavy equipment. He helped Pete fix equipment that broke down, but he's not too handy. Not like Pete," she said wistfully.

"The pump and all that hose?" Emily had spent a considerable amount of time in the warehouse.

"Squinty always hauls the chemicals, too. It's hard to use the ammonia inside a closed room without getting sick. At least, I can't. It was worse when we used ether." Beth made a gesture to dismiss such memories. "Pete always handles those things, too."

Emily looked past Beth to the road winding around the hillside. A man, hunched over and cursing his team, guided his two mules up the final incline. Even if she hadn't known this was Squinty Houseman, she would have nailed that nickname on him. His right eye was closed almost entirely shut as he drove. The left eye wandered about, not staying to the straight and narrow. In a gunfight he'd be more dangerous to those around him than in anyone standing before him.

"Howdy, Miz Randall," the man greeted. His raspy voice put Emily's nerves on edge. "Who's that?" He pointed with a finger that had been broken once too often. Whatever hell this man had been through had left him a caricature of a man.

Beth introduced them. If Squinty was unimpressed, Emily was less so. The chances of her and Beth driving the ice wagon to Tombstone themselves began rolling through her mind. She lived by odds, but whether an ace turned up to finish a royal flush was a different kind of gambling. Two women crossing New Mexico and half of Arizona driving a heavily laden wagon posed dangers beyond losing a single poker pot.

"Got more chemicals, but ain't sure you'll be needin' them," Squinty said. "Gossip's runnin' wild about Mr. Randall being one of them bank robbers. Some folks even claim it was him what gunned down Marshal Nolan." Squinty dropped to the ground, needing the wagon to support himself. Even his legs were creaky.

"I'd heard that the marshal was being buried today," Beth said. Her voice caught in her throat and tears welled but didn't spill.

"Yup, they're plantin' him in a family plot in Saint Francis Cemetery. Ain't many who dispute Mr. Randall bein' the one that gunned him down. Not at all." He shook his head. "They got a thousand-dollar reward out for him. Imagine that. A thousand dollars."

Squinty Houseman looked around, as if expecting his boss to jump from behind a bush or peek out from inside the warehouse. That much money turned a man's loyalty in jig time.

"We'll need help loading the wagon for the trip to Arizona," Emily said. Changing the subject from reward money on Pete Randall's head did nothing to divert Beth's thoughts. The tears that had built finally ran down her cheeks. She turned away to keep from showing them to the hired help.

"When you want me to head out? It'll take most of the day to secure the load. I can be on the trail by sunup."

"That sounds like a reasonable time to leave," Emily said. "How far do you think we can drive the first day?"

"We?" Squinty turned his good, if wandering, eye in her direction. "I kin handle the trip myself. No call for Miz Randall to disconvenience herself."

"I'm going," Beth said firmly.

"So am I," Emily added loudly enough to be sure that the hired hand heard.

"Ladies, the trip's mighty hazardous in the best of times. Me and Mr. Randall ran into all kinds of owlhoots last year. Why, outside of Santa Fe we was waylaid almost a day by a gang of road agents. Then we got mired down tryin' to cross the Rio Grande above Albuquerque. We shoulda driven closer. I kin remember the spot so you don't have to ex-parry-ment findin' a different place to ford. That can be downright dangerous, even if the Rio's not runnin' bank to bank from spring runoff."

"Good," Emily said. "Remember the spot where it's better to cross for this trip."

"That ford shifts year to year," Squinty said, growing perturbed. "A good year's runoff makes the river go higher. If you never seen the Rio Grande, you can't know how treacherous it is to cross."

"Then the three of us stand a better chance than a solitary driver," Emily said firmly.

"I kin make the trip on my own." The man turned sullen.

"You know the buyers in Tombstone well enough to get a good price?" Emily pressed.

"Send a telegram down introducin' me."

"Pete always did the selling by himself," Beth said. "He said last year you lit out and got drunk the minute you rolled into town. I know the buyers better than you, from everything Pete told me."

"You're gonna be in a world of danger the whole danged way," Squinty said.

"Trouble had better run the opposite direction. We're two determined women," Emily said. She put her arm around Beth's shoulders and pulled her close. In a lower voice, she said to her friend, "He wants to hijack the load. Without us along, that'd be mighty easy."

"I'm afraid you're right," Beth said. "We'll have to watch our backs."

Emily scowled as she looked at the hired hand. From the way he stared at the two of them, Squinty was going to spend most of his time watching them for an opportune time to either strand them or outright kill them and take the wagon loaded with ice.

"Drive the supply wagon around to the side and park it. We'll use the freight wagon inside the warehouse to carry the ice," Beth said. "Loading the blocks is something I know how to do."

"What should I do with a wagon full of ammonia?" Squinty scratched himself. "I kin try to sell it back to the chemist in Taos. Don't rightly know he'd be interested in refunding the full price, but since none of the tins have been opened, he should take 'em back, at least. I don't think you'd have to offer him money to take them off your hands."

"Just store it inside the warehouse," Emily said. "Time matters. It'd take you a couple days to get back to Taos, then return."

Squinty climbed back into the driver's box, grumbling to himself. He swung the small wagon around and drove to the warehouse.

"This is going to be an interesting trip," Emily said, more to herself than to her friend.

"I've got everything packed for the trip. Pete laid in the supplies before ... before ..." She choked up.

"Before he paid for them, is my guess," Emily said. "All the more reason to get on the road fast. Merchants don't like giving credit and then having their client hightail it."

"I'll see that everyone's paid, after we deliver the ice," Beth said with steely determination. "Everyone." She headed for the icehouse.

Emily followed. They had a long day's work ahead of them loading the ice.

By the time she stepped into the warehouse, Squinty had unloaded the chemicals and had unhitched the two mules. Together with the four in the stables, they had a decent team strong enough to take even steep hills while they were in the mountains. Once they reached flatter country, that big a team meant they'd make far better time.

Emily walked around to where Squinty was working to build up the sides of the ponderous freight wagon with slats stored in a pile.

"We'll put down a tarpaulin inside the wagon bed, then spread a layer of sawdust for insulation. The ice crates will go on top of that." Emily saw immediately what the procedure was. Pete Randall had left everything ready to roll, except for stacking the ice blocks in the wagon bed.

"You kin stuff the space 'tween the boxes with more sawdust. That's what in-so-lates the ice," Squinty said.

"How many crates can you fit in?" Emily tried to picture the wagon's interior once loaded and couldn't.

"A dozen crates. Each crate's got close to $200 of cargo in it," Beth said.

Mention of the value caused Squinty to perk up. Emily vowed to keep her derringer close at hand, as well as the six-gun she carried strapped to her hip. If so much firepower wasn't used to fend off Indians and road agents, she suspected it would be put to good use keeping Squinty Houseman honest.

Once prepared with the insulating tarp and sawdust, the wagon was ready for loading. Squinty worked one end of the rope while Emily and Beth went into the loft and wrestled the heavy crates with the frozen water outward. Squinty lowered each box into the wagon bed with remarkable skill for someone who was functionally blind. The dozen crates took the better part of the day to load.

"That'll do it," the man said. "I'll get the canvas top stretched above while you finish stuffin' as much sawdust between the crates as you can."

"Then we'll cover the load with more tarps," Beth said.

"Why bother with the canvas top?" Emily asked.

"It keeps off the sun," Beth told her.

"And rain kin be as bad," Squinty added. "You don't want that rainwater joinin' up with the ice. That'll melt the load quicker 'n a flea jumps off a hot griddle. I seen it happen."

"I see I have a lot to learn," Emily said. She cut off Squinty making yet another plea to drive alone. "I do know the ice is a tad lighter than if you had loaded in water."

Squinty looked at her quizzically.

"Ice floats. That means it's got to be lighter than water."

"Never thought on that, but I reckon you're right." Squinty hitched up his trousers. "Let me pull the wagon around out of the sun. The northside's shaded from both sunset and sunrise."

"I'll get some chow started for supper," Beth said. "You coming, Emily?"

"In a few minutes. I won't be long."

Beth walked away, shoulders slumped. She was close to be being defeated, but Emily knew that it was only "close." Beth would perk up once they got on the trail and the promise of a good sale for the ice lay ahead.

She headed downhill from the icehouse. The uneasy sense of being watched still bothered her. While hardly a trailsman, she knew how to look for broken twigs and crushed grass. Nothing revealed passage recently, but she did find a patch of discolored grass. She pulled it up and studied it closely.

After she ran her fingers over it, she made a face. The brownish crust was blood. Whether it came from an animal or a human was beyond her ability to guess. Deep in her gut she worried that Pete Randall had contributed to the spot.

Walking in an ever widening spiral didn't give her anything else to worry over. By the time the deep shadows formed and the sun sank behind the nearby tall mountain peaks, Beth rang the dinner bell.

Emily hiked back to the house. The day had been hectic.

Hitting the road at the break of dawn with Squinty Houseman driving the freight wagon behind a six mule team would be the start of an even more dangerous adventure. Emily squared her shoulders and went to eat. She was up to it. She had to be.

13

Frank Landry hated the cat and mouse hunt. Usually he had no trouble figuring out if he was the hunter or the hunted. For the past two days since Buck got himself shot up at the still, Frank had dodged someone—it had to be the owlhoot who had put a bullet in Buck. But as quickly as Frank found the hunter's trail, he became the hunted.

The New Mexico forest was an easy place to get lost. The thick trees blotted out the sun. The carpet of pine needles hid tracks well. More than once Frank had found himself backtracking unintentionally. He had gotten turned around when he no longer saw the sun. Out in the desert with no decent landmark he knew men tended to curve slowly to the right and never realize it.

Here, simply turning around confused his sense of direction. It was too easy to find himself in the pickle of never finding a landmark to fix on. After what seemed an eternity of wandering in circles, he found a road that looked familiar. Even then, Frank found himself suspicious that he had somehow worked himself into a trap.

Finally satisfying himself he was alone, he rode down it a quarter mile and came out at Buck's still. The sudden appearance of the familiar still made him sit a little straighter in the saddle. He had returned to the spot he wanted by sheer chance.

Frank dismounted and hobbled Barleycorn in a wooded area out of sight of the shack. He returned to the still and poked around inside. The only worthwhile thing he found was a glass jar half full of moonshine. With a contented sigh, he sank down, unscrewed the lid and took a deep sniff. He coughed at the pungent vapors rising from the jar.

"Now this is fine 'shine," he said. Before he sampled it, a voice called out to him.

"Best I ever did, if I say so myself." Buck hobbled to the shed door and leaned against the wall. "It's got to be good if it brung you all the way back here."

Buck had startled him but he didn't dare show it. He lifted the jar in silent toast to the moonshiner, took a sip and shuddered. It was potent. He held out the jar. Buck took it, swirled the amber fluid around a couple times, then took a healthy pull on it. He smacked his lips, looked longingly at what remained, then handed it back.

Frank took it but didn't immediately sample more. His head spun from the first sip. If he took a second, he might pass out.

"I've been dodging the law," Frank said. "I think it's the law. If it isn't, then whoever shot you up is still on the warpath after me."

"Ain't any Injun, that's for sure," Buck said. He sank to the floor and thrust his legs out in front of him. "I don't sell to them, no matter how much they beg."

"It's a white man. Did you recognize the varmint that put a slug in you?" Frank pointed to Buck's bandaged head. Jenny had done a good job patching him up.

"Didn't," Buck allowed. "I've asked around thinkin' a new still operator might be responsible. As far as I can tell, there are fewer now, not more. And I know every solitary soul amongst them. Not a one of 'em has got the sand to try to kill me." He accepted the jar and drained the contents with a belch. "That is mighty fine liquor. Yes, sir, you're gonna get the best there is in these here hills." He cocked his head to the side. His eyes had blurred a little from the sudden downing of so much moonshine. "That is, if you're still in the market."

"How closely is the marshal watching you?"

Buck laughed. "Don't take it wrong, Mr. Landry, Jenny putting him on you trail like she done."

"She did what was necessary," Frank said. "We'd all have ended up dead if Babson had twigged to what was going on between you and Jenny."

"That makes it kinda excitin'," Buck admitted. "Jasper is a wet blanket. I don't blame her for findin' me more to her taste. That gal's a real pistol."

"What do you hear about the law catching the bank robbers?"

Buck shook his head. He ran his finger around inside the jar rim and sucked on his finger to savor the very last drop.

"Sheriff Thompson has a real burr under his saddle," he finally said. "Somebody down in Santa Fe is pokin' him like a grizzly bear in an iron cage. Marshal Nolan don't mean squat to them. Local law dogs are a dime a dozen. It's all about Jaime Ochoa gettin' ventilated. Mark my words, that's what's got 'em so stirred up."

"Politics," Frank said. Buck nodded.

They sat quietly, surrounded by the distilling equipment and empty jars. Somewhere along the way Frank had lost his sample case. The whiskey in it would go a ways toward quenching his thirst. Running for his life took a toll on a man and gave a powerful thirst.

"'Bout everybody knows it was Pete Randall what killed the marshal. Maybe the banker, too. The others with him, well, three of them are dead. Until Pete and the other one's brung down, the sheriff ain't gonna rest easy."

"I need to contact some of my principals," Frank said. He found a scrap of paper and the nub of a pencil he'd used often to write orders for his company's whiskey. "Can you see that this telegram is sent?"

"Don't see why not, if it brings in the money to fill that fifty-gallon order you made. I'm lookin' forward to runnin' that out. Ain't never cooked up a batch that big. I'm takin' it as a challenge—if you can actually pay for it." Buck remained skeptical, and Frank didn't blame him. Such an order had to be greater than all he'd distilled since setting up his operation.

"It's in code. Don't worry if you can't understand it. The man receiving it will understand."

Buck peered at the neatly written message.

"This Augustus Crane gent. He's a postmaster up in Denver?"

"He's in contact with my backer." Frank thought it was safer sending the 'gram to the postmaster since he funneled most of the communications for the Society of Buckhorn and Bison. Getting the information to Allister Legende would be a snap for him and saved Frank the need to anger Legende if he took umbrage at having one of his agents mixed up in local politics.

And there was more than that involved.

Legende had assigned Emily to find Jaime Ochoa's killer, not Frank Landry. Frank was dealing himself in and pointed out how Emily had failed, so far. While this wasn't his concern, he felt the need for a little one-upmanship. Legende favored Frank's ex-wife a bit too much.

"But he didn't know I was already in New Mexico," Frank muttered.

"How's that?" Buck looked up. "You say something?"

"There's a woman poking around. Bright red hair, eyes so green they look like emeralds in the sunlight. You know who I mean?"

"Heard that she and Beth Randall are friendly. Makes you wonder, don't it?"

Frank waited for Buck to continue.

"This woman gambler from Santa Fe and the wife of the man who's accused of robbing the bank being all tight. I hesitate to say they're thicker 'n thieves."

Frank sucked in his breath. That must be why Legende had sent Emily. She and Pete Randall's wife were friends. He almost asked Buck to destroy the message intended for Legende. Then he came to a different decision.

"The icehouse is owned by Randall. You think he'll try to get back there to see his wife?"

Buck nodded knowingly.

Frank heaved to his feet. "Get that telegram sent off when you can. Here." He fished around in a vest pocket until he found a silver cartwheel.

"This might be too much," Buck said.

That surprised Frank. The man was a moonshiner and committed adultery with the marshal's wife. Those were just the things Frank knew about. And yet he worried that he'd received too much money.

"Get yourself a shot of tequila with whatever's left."

"Might be enough for two."

"Buy one for Jenny, too," Frank said. "If that doesn't get you both into hot water."

Buck laughed. "We kinda enjoy sloshin' around in that boilin' water. Makes us both feel alive."

They shook hands. Buck looked around with some longing, then left. He moved slowly. His wound bothered him more than he let on, but he had come out to his still. That told Frank of the man's determination to begin producing moonshine again.

Rather than follow immediately, Frank stayed in the shed and watched the forest for any sign of pursuers. Falling into a trap now was the last thing he wanted to do after sending Buck off with note to Allister Legende bragging on how well he could handle the Society's assignment.

Finally sure nothing lurked in the forest, he went and unhobbled Barleycorn. The horse hadn't finished nibbling at the dried grass but put up little complaint as he rode away from the still and found the road leading higher into the mountains. Before he'd gone two miles he saw the sign with chipped paint lettering letting him know he was on his way to the High Lonesome Ice Company.

He tried to put a face to the name Randall. While it had been years since he and Emily divorced, he thought he knew most of her friends. Pete Randall's wife might be a recent acquisition and Frank knew the woman by a different name. If that was the case, only talking with her would spark a memory. Or she and Emily might have been friends before he even met his former wife. Not for the first time he realized how little he knew of the woman's background other than her family damned near owned Boston and she had traveled widely on their money.

Whether he should even try to strike up a conversation with Beth Randall was a different matter. He wrestled with announcing himself to Emily but came to no decision by the time the icehouse poked above the pines. Across a large yard stood a house. The first thing he noticed was the lack of smoke curling from the chimney.

"Nobody home, old friend," he said, patting the horse on the neck. "Let's see what they've left behind that we can use."

Right away he found a shed where four mules had been stabled. A battered gray canvas nosebag brimmed with grain. Frank had a hard time getting it onto his gelding's head. The horse was too eager for grain after a steady diet of dried grass for the past week. Finally settling the straps around Barleycorn's ears, he backed away, then cautiously went to the icehouse.

The pump was silent. No water was brought uphill from a small lake. Pungent fumes made his nose wrinkle. The ammonia odor was even more pronounced when he went inside.

The interior was close to pitch black. Only a few rays of sunlight angled through cracks in the walls. He wandered about, not sure what he sought. A ladder at one end of high-walled vats led him to the rickety catwalk.

The lighting here was somewhat better than below. He edged along the planks, clutching the rope railing with enough intensity to cramp his forearms. Looking down into the vats caused a hint of vertigo. He counted where a dozen of the ice coffins had been removed. The few at the far end of the warehouse held half-frozen water.

Working his way down one plank wall, he prowled the empty vat not sure what he sought. A large scrap of paper had been torn away and lodged in a crack in the wall. Frank glanced at it but the hen scratching on it meant nothing. It took him a few more minutes to explore the empty bottom before giving up.

"How to get out of here," he said, looking up at the ten-foot wall he had descended from the catwalk.

The problem was solved when he saw how the operators mastered the wall. A knotted rope dangled in one corner. Boots against the wall, hands gripping the knots, he walked his way up to the catwalk. As flimsy as it was, he was glad to be out of the vat and able to reach the ladder at the end. Being in the wood box was too much like finding himself in a huge grave.

When he stepped from the icehouse into the sunlight rapidly disappearing over a tall peak to the west, he realized only one place remained unexplored. Frank went to the house and knocked on the door. The only sound he heard was the wind rustling the tall pines at the rear of the house. He stepped inside.

As he suspected, the occupants were gone, but not too long ago.

"Time to make myself at home." He laid a fire in the stove and hunted through the larder for something to eat. By the time he'd eaten, he was feeling mellow and ready for a good night's sleep.

He stretched out on the first comfortable bed he'd found since coming to New Mexico.

"Oh, Emily, did you sleep here, too?"

Frank Landry drifted off to sleep with images of his ex-wife dancing in his head.

14

Dandy Dan Dinkins burned his finger on the hot griddle on top of the stove. He sucked on it, glad it wasn't his trigger finger. Someone had definitely been here. From the way everything had been neatly cleaned and returned to cabinets, he wasn't sure if it was Randall's wife doing the housekeeping or the moonshiner he trailed.

He paced around, munching on an old sourdough biscuit he had found in a jar. All the jams were gone. Their empty bottles suggested someone had purposefully finished them off rather than leave them behind.

Nothing had gone right. His scheme for using two bodies to decoy Sheriff Thompson had exploded in his face. Back at the still he'd been sure one of the moonshiners was dead by his hand. But after failing to track down the fancy dressed one who fled and eventually slipped away from him, he had returned to the still thinking to claim one body. Only a bloody patch of ground showed where the body should have been. A quick search of the area hadn't turned up a fresh grave.

So the two bodies he needed to get Thompson off his trail

had disappeared. Both of them. His luck continued to drain away.

"Randall's got to be around here somewhere. He's got to be," Dinkins said loudly, as if daring the walls to argue with him. All he heard was a faint echo of his own words and the restless wind blowing through the tall Ponderosa pines.

He kicked the door shut behind him and stalked across the wide yard to the icehouse. He had killed one woman who had tried to stop him from searching the warehouse. At least he saw no way she had survived a fall into the vat. He had watched her break through the ice and then sink out of sight. He wasn't sure who she was.

With his increasingly awful luck, that might have been Randall's wife. Any chance of using her as bait to flush out the only robber to end up with the loot from the robbery was frozen stiff.

Dinkins rubbed his nose and sneezed. The pungent ammonia stench was stronger than before. He climbed the ladder to the catwalk and slowly went down the entire length. Most of the big vats were empty now. He frowned. That meant someone had loaded them onto a wagon and pulled out. He went to the far end and saw the ice coffin where he had dumped the woman was gone.

"So somebody's got a block of ice with a dead body in it." He decided they didn't know. He laughed aloud at that. It was the only funny thing that had happened in days. He imagined what the reception would be when the ice block's buyer began chipping away for his customers.

A hand? A foot? What would be revealed first? Knowing most barkeeps as he did, Dinkins knew the ice wouldn't be discarded because of mere bodily contamination. The ice would be chipped away and the body discarded before it thawed. In some saloons the frozen body might be put on display for a dime a peek. In others even more depraved, the bar owner might charge a dollar for even more heinous uses.

Dinkins started to figure out a way to climb back when he saw a scrap of paper struck between two boards. Gently teasing it out, he held it up and tried to make heads or tails of it. Then his eyes lit up and he let out a yell of glee.

"A map. Randall, you double-crossing, son of a mangy dog, you made a map of where you stashed the loot." He examined the torn paper more closely. "Or was it you, Hugh Wilson?"

The paper had been taken from the bank. He recognized the letterhead, what there was of it. Beneath the embossed lettering stretched lines and an arrow. Part of a word remained.

"Blue? What's that supposed to mean? Wilson was from around here. What's named Blue?" Dinkins paced back and forth wracking his brain. Without the rest of the map, he had nothing more to go on.

Randall had taken the map from the dying Hugh Wilson. Or he had killed Wilson for the map?

"Then Randall came here," Dinkins said, looking around the wooden walls of the ice vat. "But there's no way he gave it to his wife. Not with the sheriff prowling about."

The other woman bothered him. She had been here for a reason before he killed her by dumping her into the ice. Was she a courier with the map? Randall might have given it to her for his wife.

He shook his head. That made no sense. Every time he had found Randall's blood-soaked trail, he had been trying to return to the icehouse. Carrying a map made sense if Sheriff Thompson caught him. It was easier to destroy the map to where the loot had been buried than it was dumping a bag of greenbacks and gold coins. Whether the sheriff cared much about the money was a question Dinkins avoided.

Randall should never have shot the banker, Dinkins regretted gunning down the marshal but he'd had no choice. But who had shot Wilson? Was that the Chandler brothers' doing? Who had pulled the trigger during their wild escape didn't matter now. The law wasn't going to stop hunting for the culprits until they found someone to string up.

"Get the map, get the loot, get the hell out of New Mexico Territory!" The words came easily to his lips. It seemed easy enough, only no part of that simple plan was going to get done just like that.

He snapped his fingers and stared at his hand.

"Where's the rest of the map?" He searched the vat and thought about checking the others. Then Dinkins realized Randall had no reason to split the map between ice vats. This piece had torn off in his haste to ... to do what with the map?

"Into a block of ice. He froze the map. And a dozen crates of ice are gone."

Dinkins found the knotted rope and painfully pulled himself up. He wasn't used to such exertion. He sat on the edge of the vat, looking down to where the ice blocks had been frozen before being loaded into a wagon and hauled off to who knew where.

He hurried from the icehouse and mounted his horse. Deep ruts from a heavily loaded freighter showed the direction taken from the High Lonesome Ice Company. He raked the sides of his horse to keep it moving. He had a map to recover and a fortune to claim!

TWO DAYS. TWO MISERABLE, LONG DAYS AND HE HADN'T come up with a decent plan. Dandy Dan Dinkins had overtaken the heavily laden ice wagon pulled by its team of six mules by noon the day after he had searched the icehouse. He

GUNSMOKE AND ICE

pressed his hand into the pocket where the scrap of paper rested—the partial map showing where the bank money had been buried.

But he had expected to spot Pete Randall riding with the wagon. Or at least trailing it. The past few hours had resurrected Dinkins' notion that the map was frozen in one of the blocks of ice and Randall's corpse clutched it tightly. That meant two blocks of ice carried corpses.

During the first night he had crept close and looked into the wagon. He counted a dozen wood crates of ice, heavily insulated with sawdust and canvas tarps. What he sought might be hidden in any of the ice blocks.

Worst of all, from spying on the two women as they whispered around the campfire, he doubted either had so much as a hint what they carried along with the ice.

Dinkins walked closer on cat's feet. It was less than an hour before sunrise. Santa Fe was definitely the destination and from there they had discussed various routes down to Arizona. The driver with the wandering eye and perpetual squint claimed to know the quickest way, having made the trip before.

If it hadn't been for him, Dinkins would have boldly walked into their camp, six-shooter drawn and chased them off so he could open and examine the caskets of ice. One thing prevented him from trying it.

The driver never let a rifle get more than a foot or two away. He even slept with it, arms and legs curled around its cold steel length as if it were some kind of perverse lover.

"Shoot him," Dinkins said to himself. "Just go on in, shoot him and those women will cry and faint and I can chip out the map." He heaved a sigh. He had to find the map first. After he got rid of the trio guarding the ice shipment, that wouldn't be difficult at all.

He slid his six-gun from its holster, spun it around his

index finger using the trigger guard in a flashy, defiant move and started for the camp.

Dinkins froze when he heard a metallic click behind him. Too many times he had been the one cocking a six-shooter to mistake the distinctive sound for anything else. Soft footfalls warned someone crept up on him. Letting his knees lower him, he dropped to the ground and rolled beside a dead log. His iron came up to cover his back trail. Anyone there trying to back shoot him would discover how he'd turned the tables.

His lungs threatened to explode when he held his breath too long. He sat up abruptly, not caring if the movement drew fire. He wasn't a patient man. Lying in wait to ambush whoever stalked him wasn't his style.

"Who's out there?"

Dinkins glanced over his shoulder toward the guttering campfire. The driver moaned and thrashed about as nightmares filled his head. Across the fire, barely visible in the low light, one of the women also stirred. Dim firelight reflected off a six-gun. The other woman was nowhere to be seen.

"Come on out, honey chile. I got what you're lookin' for."

Dinkins got his feet under him and duck walked back.

A shadow darted away, going deeper into the wood. He homed in on the movement. His plan of getting the drop on all three as they slept seemed naive now. If they had awakened in surprise, they'd have fired at anything moving. He had completely missed how the third one with the freight wagon was out patrolling the perimeter. How he had missed her as he made his way to the fire was a poser.

He had missed her in the dense, dark forest. She had missed him. Only now he knew where she was, and it didn't seem that she had spotted him.

He didn't cotton to gunning down a woman, but he would. The stakes were too high to have any qualms about such a thing now.

The dark figure moving ahead of him slowed. Dinkins got ready to fire. He drew a bead and then had a prickly sensation up and down his spine. Half turning, he saw another shadow hurtling for him. They crashed down to the forest floor, each struggling to get on top. Dinkins lost his pistol and clutched at a sinewy wrist holding a Colt.

With a mighty heave as he arched his back, Dinkins threw his attacker aside. He scrambled to find his dropped gun. By the time his fingers curled around the butt, he knew he was in serious trouble. Whoever had jumped him was gone, but the woman from camp let out a cry of warning.

She blundered toward him. He heard the other woman waking the man who slept with his rifle held so closer. Over the din, Dinkins turned to ice when he heard the rifle cocking. He faced the three driving the ice wagon as well as a mysterious man who had jumped him.

Flinging lead all around served no purpose other than to show everyone where he was from the muzzle flashes. Dinkins rolled over a rock, crashed through undergrowth and then twisted this way and that through the dense forest until he had left everyone behind.

Everyone, he hoped, including whoever had jumped him from behind before he had a chance to gun down the woman sentry. More planning was needed before he retrieved the map Pete Randall had taken with him to his icy grave.

15

Frank Landry rode at a steady clip, following the narrow dirt track where he discovered the deep ruts caused by the recent passage of a heavy wagon. The mountains were deserted at this time of year. This had to be the High Lonesome Ice Company freight wagon.

The warm sun on his face let him drift a mite as he trotted along. His mind tumbled about and plans formed, only to crumble as fast as they grew. He had no idea why he stuck his nose into Emily's assignment. Allister Legende had chosen her for a reason.

"She was already in Santa Fe," he said aloud, trying to make sense of it. "That's good enough a reason. And he had no idea I was anywhere nearby. Otherwise, he would have sent me to find whoever killed Jaime Ochoa. I'm obviously a better choice than Emily for such a job."

That's what Frank told himself, and it carried a ring of truth to it. Whatever background Emily had received from Legende gave her a more complete assignment, but some things bothered him.

How was she supposed to catch anybody on the trail

south to Santa Fe riding alongside a freighter? In a wagon creaking under the weight of a dozen crates filled with ice? The dead bank president and the shot up marshal were all back in Taos. Using the shipment as some sort of bait made no sense. Nothing Emily did made any sense to him.

He smiled wryly. While they were married, he had the same problem.

Listening to the moonshiner relay gossip around Taos, Pete Randall was widely accepted as the one who had gunned down both Jaime Ochoa and Marshal Nolan. For all Frank knew, he was also responsible for killing all the other robbers. Buck hadn't been certain of how many had taken part in the heist. Four or five?

Sheriff Thompson knew, but Frank wasn't in any position to ask the law dog or any of his posse. The sheriff was as inclined to toss him in the calaboose as he was to divulge any information. More than that, he and his men still roamed the Sangre de Cristos hunting for the robbers.

Frank had to smile when he considered his bad luck with Marshal Babson. If the lawman's wife hadn't needed to cover up her affair with the moonshiner, he would have been on the wrong side of the bars in the Taos jailhouse for a long time. Jenny was, as Buck declared, a pistol. A tiny shiver crept up Frank's spine thinking about the trouble he'd be in if he and Jenny had shared more than a fleeting touch.

For her, it was exciting. For him, he could have ended up being slaughtered in Jasper Babson's cell.

Most of all he wondered if Buck had sent the telegram to Denver and Augustus Crane. Gus was old and moved around as if he'd fall apart at any instant. Frank knew the postmaster was tougher than he looked and a considerable bit smarter than anyone's first impression declared.

"Will Legende be mad that I'm cutting into Emily's assignment? Or is finding Ochoa's killer more important than hurt feelings?" He patted his gelding's neck and asked, "What's your opinion, Barleycorn?" As often happened, the horse saw fit to give him the silent treatment. That in its way was answer enough.

He shouldn't have interfered, but he was already too involved to back out.

"So what do you think? Should I announce myself and ride along openly beside Emily? Or should I trail the wagon and keep an eye peeled for trouble sneaking up on her? Go on, old friend. What's your opinion?"

This time the gelding neighed loudly and shook its head vigorously. It might have intended to swish its mane about to rid itself of annoying flies or it could have been giving its opinion.

Frank interpreted it as the latter. Arguing with Emily constantly served neither of them. It certainly did nothing to catch Jaime Ochoa's murderer. If Emily had a plan, let it reel out. Frank's trusty Colt Navy provided plenty of firepower to back up any trouble she got herself into.

If history was any guide, she'd end up in hot water before too much longer.

He took a deep whiff of the nighttime air and caught the scent of burning oak. Emily had camped not too far ahead. Frank dismounted and rummaged through his saddlebags. What little food he had there was jerky and old biscuits hard enough to crack a tooth on. He had other provender, but it required building a fire to prepare. Worse of all was the lack of coffee. A steamy cup of Arbuckle's right now would chase away the chill. If he hadn't lost his sample case, a drop or two of fine whiskey would have made it all go down his gullet more equitably.

As it was, lumps formed in his chest. He massaged out the stuck food and belched. When he had finished his simple cold meal he leaned back and closed his eyes. They snapped open after what seemed a few seconds, but from the moonlight filtering through the tall pines, he had slept more than a couple hours.

Barleycorn nickered wetly and tugged on his bridle. Frank paid attention now. His horse had keener hearing than he did.

He slid his six-shooter from the holster and went toward Emily's camp, careful not to make any sound. Blundering in on her was a sure way to get filled full of lead. He had no idea how itchy her traveling companions' trigger fingers were, but he knew her. While it was hardly her motto to live by, she figured it was better to shoot first and explain later. She was good enough with both her derringer and a rifle that she seldom had to explain.

Corpses didn't care.

Frank pressed against a thick tree trunk and tried to hide entirely behind it. A shadowy figure crept past. From the hints he got, this wasn't Emily. Someone tried to sneak up on her camp.

And then a ruckus broke out. He had been right about Emily standing guard. She never hailed the man or made silly demands to know who was there. Anyone creeping around the forest in the dead of night wasn't up to any good.

Frank smiled, just a little. Nobody was up to any good unless it was him. He was out here to protect her. Then he smiled even more broadly. He was out her to show her up. Legende had sent her to find the banker's killer. He had no qualms about letting his ex-wife do all the work and then taking credit.

Muffled words were exchanged. Frank knew they weren't pleasantries. Emily and the stalker fought. He slid his six-gun out and rushed forward. The man attacking Emily O'Connor had her pinned to the ground and tried to draw his iron.

Frank swung his pistol and caught Emily's attacker on the

side of the head. He went flying. Before Frank could call out, Emily twisted away and grabbed for her rifle.

Her attacker stumbled off, and she levered in a round, ready to open fire. Frank lit out after the fleeing man. Whoever that was had answers to questions. For all he knew, this might give Allister Legende all the information he needed to solve the question of who gunned down Jaime Ochoa. At the very least, Frank could make the man reveal why he was secretly trailing Emily and the ice freighter.

A rifle bullet tore past him and sang off into the night. He wanted to tell Emily she targeted the wrong one. Then he reconsidered. Sowing such confusion only made matters worse. He grinned crookedly. For all he knew, she might prefer to put a bullet in him rather than the man who had been trailing her.

He ducked, dodged and drew up behind a tree out of sight to catch his breath. Emily called out for him—for someone—to surrender. He wasn't going to do that. She was so angry at being jumped she'd shoot anyone trying to surrender.

And her attacker was running through the woods like a frightened rabbit. Frank decided this was a sensible course to follow.

Leaving Emily behind, he slowly followed the man who had attacked Emily. When he heard hoofbeats, he knew he had a chase on his hands. He got his bearings, retrieved his horse and finally got on the track. If luck held, his quarry wouldn't run too far. Then Frank could get a decent idea of what was going on.

He might even deliver Jaime Ochoa's killer to Legende before his ex-wife figured out she had let the owlhoot slip through her fingers. That made the pursuit all the more invigorating.

16

"This part is the roughest we'll hit. The rest of the way's on better road." Squinty Houseman didn't convince Emily.

"Once we get past Albuquerque, you're saying the Jornado del Muerto is *easier*?"

"Well, now, it's all a matter of what we gotta face. This time of year, runoffs starting so we got plenny of water in the Rio Grande. We won't have to scrounge around for water and suck on prickly pear pads to keep from dyin' of thirst."

"That also means more merchants traveling. You're probably right that the heat's not as bad now as it will be in a few weeks, but road agents will be plying their trade," Emily said.

"Don't know 'bout them plyin' anything, but we don't have a cargo worth hijackin'. If we was one of the Butterfield stagecoaches creakin' under the weight of too much gold, we'd be in trouble."

Emily rode closer to the wagon. Beth Randall stared ahead. Her pale face was an emotionless mask, and she might have been a waxen statue for all the movement she betrayed.

"Is that the way it is, Beth?" Emily discounted Squinty's

appraisal and wouldn't have pursued the matter further if she hadn't wanted to see some spark of life in her friend. The last time she remembered Beth speaking was after they rolled through Santa Fe.

Since then she had been as quiet as a church mouse.

"He's not wrong," Beth finally said.

"It's taken us four days to get past Santa Fe. It'll be another day or two into Albuquerque."

"Quicker after that," Beth said, as if repeating Squinty's words. "Once we get to Silver City and over the Continental Divide, it's nothing but desert roads."

"That'll be hotter. Won't the ice melt faster?"

Beth nodded.

"If 'n it suits you, why not stay in Albuquerque?" Squinty turned his head slightly so his wall-eye stared at Emily. "You might even want to get on back to Santa Fe. You got friends there, don't you?"

"Why do you say that?"

"Well, now, you came on up to the icehouse from there. You weren't in Taos when all the shootin' went on. It was like somebody tole you 'bout it all and you left your business behind."

Emily heard the unspoken *and came to stick your nose where it doesn't belong*.

"I worried that Beth—Mrs. Randall—needed some help. It looks as if I was right."

"Not sure what help you're affordin' her," the hired hand said sourly.

"Who's been trailing us since we left the icehouse?"

Squinty jerked around. For a moment his wandering eye took in different scenery, then settled back on Emily.

"What are you goin' on about? Who's after us?"

"Don't you know?" She felt a pang of disappointment when she saw that Squinty didn't know. His reaction was honest enough to make her think he hadn't any idea of them being tracked.

"The other night," he said. "You shot at somebody doggin' us?"

Emily hadn't elaborated about the fight where she had gotten away from her attacker. Or were there two of them? In the dark she wasn't sure. The one she had wrestled to the ground had lit a shuck when she fired at him. She had expected to target his partner, only there wasn't any sure sign of a second man.

"Are those telegraph wires?" She pointed to a nearby ridge.

"We're close to town," Beth said. "Reckon they must be."

"I need to send a message. Find a spot to camp for the night. I'll send my telegram and be back as fast as I can."

"We're still a few miles out. Ride on into town, why don't you, and we'll keep rollin' 'til sundown. Every mile counts when you got ice meltin'," Squinty said.

Emily chewed at her lower lip, thinking about this. What he said made sense, but she didn't want to ride off and then lose track of where Squinty and Beth had driven.

"There's a road under the wires once we get closer to Albuquerque," Beth said. "We'll travel that way. You won't have any trouble finding us."

Emily felt uneasy about this but sending a telegram to Allister Legende was the least she could do after vanishing from Taos. While it strained her imagination thinking Legende was frantic over her safety—he was too cool and collected to be worried—it was still her duty to keep him informed. How she would word the telegram to make it seem that she was still on the Society assignment would be a major work of fiction.

She might just let him know she'd lit out for Tombstone

with a wagon laden with ice blocks and to hell with the mission.

She might say that, but she wouldn't.

"All right," she said. "When you hit the road head on toward town. I'll ride as fast as I can and meet you before sundown."

"More like midnight," Squinty said. "This is rough country. Even the potholes in the road's got holes in 'em. You might consider ridin' beside the road. We got to follow the ruts."

Emily discarded what Squinty had to say. This time it sounded as if he was pulling her leg, only there wasn't any humor in it. She tapped her heels on her horse's flanks and galloped off. Within two miles she found a road. The telegraph lines overheard assured her she was on the right track. Within an hour she topped a rise and stared down into a rocky bowl holding Albuquerque. Keeping the wires overhead led her to a telegraph office near the train station just off Railroad Avenue.

She dismounted, stretched the kinks out of her shoulders and went inside. The doors and windows were open although it was a brisk day. The moving air kept the fumes from the lead-sulfuric acid batteries from becoming overpowering. A thin man with a hatchet face and green eye shades worked diligently transferring code from a piece of foolscap to an official looking telegram form.

"What can I do for you, Missy?" The man never looked up.

"Denver. A telegram to the postmaster." Emily finally got the man's attention.

"By the name of Augustus Crane?"

"Do you know Gus?" She watched his eyes harden as he studied her.

"Only because the postmaster of any big town gets a lot of traffic."

"Society traffic?" she asked as casually as possible.

"Don't know about that. What's the message?" He pushed aside his work and took out a pad of paper. He touched the tip of the pencil to his tongue to wet the graphite, then waited.

All the way into town she had written and rewritten the message destined for Legende. He'd know where she sent the telegram so there wasn't any need to mention that.

"Here it is: Following cold trail. Hope it heats up soon."

"That's all? Hardly worth the effort tapping it out," the telegrapher said. He tore off the page and went to a desk where his telegraph key had been nailed to the top. Using his foot, he hooked a chair leg and pulled it under him. Intent now, he spent less than twenty seconds sending the dits-and-dahs.

A single click came back. He leaned back and looked up at Emily. "The message's sent. Gus will get it within the hour."

"How much do I owe you?"

He hesitated, then smiled. It wasn't a pleasant look, but Emily wasn't going to argue when he said, "Too short a message to charge you for it. You waiting for a reply?"

"No," she said. "Business takes me away. Back on the trail."

"Where are you heading?"

Emily knew this information would be sent along to Gus and forwarded to Legende, no matter how she cautioned the telegrapher. If he wasn't a member of the Society of Buckhorn and Bison, he was beholden to Legende in some fashion.

"To catch a killer," she said. Emily wasn't the least bit surprised that the telegrapher only nodded knowingly, as if a woman traveling alone told him such things all the time. This convinced her he was a flunky of Legende, at least as much as Augustus Crane was.

The telegrapher nodded slowly, then said, "There's reports of Apache raiders out west of Silver City. Keep an eye peeled out there on the trail. The cavalry's 'bout got 'em rounded up, but a few of the varmints always escape. Look at Geronimo and his band."

Emily thanked him, wondering about his response. Then she shrugged it off. She had done her duty to the Society, as she saw it. Now she felt a load off her shoulders. Devoting her time completely to helping Beth wouldn't interfere with her assignment. Before she left town, she purchased a few more boxes of ammo for her rifle. She had the feeling the rounds would come in handy before they reached Tombstone.

She rode more slowly back down the road. Her horse was tired and so was she. It gave her a chance to consider things other than pleasing Allister Legende. When she topped a rise in the road she saw where Squinty had pulled off the road and had made camp for the night near a small stream feeding into the Rio Grande.

Emily sat and watched the backtrail. A single rifle shot wasn't enough to scare off a determined man, but what was he determined to do? Spying on the ice wagon wasn't too useful. All it took was for a quick glance under a tarp to see what the cargo was. Any self-respecting road agent would want gold or other valuables for the effort of running down a victim to rob.

She sat a tad straighter in the saddle when a silvery glint caught her eye. The setting sun had reflected off metal. She shielded her eyes to stare into the sunset. Movement was all she made out. There might have been a solitary rider spying on Beth's camp.

"Or two men," she said softly. Chances were good she hadn't run off whoever followed them. She reached down and touched the stock of her rifle. She was a good shot but the distance was too great. The six-shooter riding at her hip was even less useful.

Rather than join Beth and Squinty as they set up camp, she circled wide and came up on a sparsely wooded patch where she had spotted the snoops. The bosque was quiet. Too quiet. She dismounted and began a careful study of the ground. A sliver of moon had risen over the mountains to the east of town and cast silvery light to help her hunt.

She dropped to her knees and ran her finger around what might have been a fresh hoofprint. She looked toward the camp where she had a good view of Beth working to prepare supper. Squinty tended the mules. The wagon was clearly visible. If someone had stood here, they had seen everything there was to be seen.

Emily worked back into the cottonwoods until she found another partial hoofprint. She drew the six-shooter holstered at her hip but didn't cock it. The sound would carry in the still night. If whoever had spied on Beth and the ice wagon still lurked, Emily didn't want to warn them. When she got the drop on them, that was plenty of time to cock and fire.

"Indians," she said softly, remembering what the telegrapher had said. Nothing had been said in Santa Fe about raiders going off their reservations, but she hadn't paid much attention. Then she had been consumed with finding decent poker games. And then Legende had nudged her away from her profession. "Indians," she repeated.

This was the first credible threat she'd heard from someone who might be affiliated with the Society. But she shivered as she remembered whoever had dumped her into the ice coffin. He hadn't been an Indian.

She kept hunting for some clue as to tracked the wagon and spied on them. The trees thinned out and an open, sandy stretch gave her a better look at the trail. A single rider, one horse. She waited as the moon climbed higher in the black velvet sky to examine the tracks more closely.

"It's possible an Indian stole a shod horse," she said. "It's more likely that whoever tried to kill me is still on our trail."

The clearest hoofprints showed distinct horseshoe impressions. While not all Indians rode unshod mounts, she decided this was the simpler solution. Emily mounted and retraced the path to where Beth had camped. By the time she arrived, Beth had cooked dinner in a Dutch oven and Squinty worked on what was his second helping.

"You made it just in time," Beth said. "Squinty was working up the nerve to polish off what's left of the stew. The biscuits are already gone."

"I'll survive," Emily said, settling down at the fire. More than once she looked over her shoulder in the direction of where someone had spied on them. She'd have to be more vigilant to keep from getting ambushed.

17

Emily slept uneasily all night. She jumped at ordinary sounds and prowled about restlessly. No matter how hard she tried to pierce the shroud of night around the camp, she never saw anything moving. Not even a rabbit or deer. By the time dawn lit the sky over the mountains to the east, she almost wished she had tangled with a bear or mountain lion. Those fierce creatures would have justified her edginess.

As Squinty Houseman went about fixing their morning meal, she asked, "Have you heard anything about an Apache war party in the area?"

He looked up at her, his screwed-shut eye trying to fix on her. He finally shook his head.

"Can't rightly say that I have. Not recently. A year back some drifted over from the Llano Estacado. They might have been Comanches from around Adobe Wells, I recollect. Or Lipan. But the Navajos drove 'em out within a few weeks. Or maybe it was the Utes. They raid down from Colorado into this area now and again. Fierce warriors, no matter that Chief Ouray's signed some kind of peace treaty."

His answer did nothing to ease her nerves. If Indians weren't after them, then the man who'd tried to kill her back at the icehouse was the next best guess. The evidence of a shod horse lent some truth to that. And all she had found was a single horse's hoofprints. A band of Indians would have left more. Lots more. And following them seemed like a poor tactic for a renegade band pursued by the cavalry. They'd look for quick strikes and fast retreats.

"Somebody put a burr under your saddle about Injuns?"

"What? No," she said, too hastily. "Well, I sent a telegram."

"And the telegrapher spun some wild yarns about scalpin' savages runnin' roughshod? Them townsfolk love to spook greenhorns."

She almost blurted that she wasn't a tenderfoot, then held back the fierce words. Squinty wanted to rile her. Or scare her off. He had done nothing to win her trust in the few days they'd been on the trail.

"The cargo's looking good," Beth Randall said, inadvertently breaking the tension. She rounded the wagon and wiped her hands off on her skirts. Dark hand prints remained. She paid them no attention.

"Not much melting?" Emily guessed.

"Not a drop. Not so far, but that'll change when we get rolling fast and hit some desert down at lower elevations."

"It's beginning to look like desert here," Emily said. She remembered how sandy it had been going to Albuquerque. The mountains to the east of town were still capped with snow and some peaks farther south looked like they had yet to contribute to spring runoff, but west of town stretched a high mesa and sand all the way to the horizon. Not a bit of that expanse showed any lingering ice or snow.

"We follow the river, then cut across around Fort Craig and head southwest for Silver City. After we get across the continental divide there, it's real desert," Beth said. "We drive as hard and as long every day that we can because nothing'll stop the sun from melting the whole load."

"I heard tell of some freighters fastening tin across the top of their wagons. It makes them like a mirror. That robs the sun of some heat, but I don't know why." Squinty stared into a tin plate and studied his own reflection, then began passing around the plates.

Emily hunkered down and ate in silence. She wanted to tell Beth what she had seen returning from town but not while Squinty was in earshot. The chance to warn her of someone following them disappeared when they finished. Emily cleaned the plates and cups. It'd be her turn to fix supper that night and Beth would clean up. The division of labor kept any of them from getting disgusted with a single chore, but it took away from Emily's efforts to flush their stalker.

Somehow, telling Squinty to be on the lookout seemed wrong, if not downright dangerous. Besides, he was the best one to drive the wagon and tend the cantankerous mule team. Together, she and Beth might have coped, but having a man in the driver's box went a ways toward preventing the six balky creatures from simply stopping or, worse, running away.

A strong muleskinner's whip kept them under control.

"I'll ride ahead and scout," Emily said suddenly. Her apprehension almost reached a boiling point, and she couldn't put her finger on why. This sense gave her an edge in a poker game on whether to fold, bluff or raise. It might just keep them alive now.

"Not much to scout on this section. We've got a solid road now and can make better time. Tryin' to cut our own road through the forest up in the Sangres was the hard part of the trip." Squinty peered at her. "Other 'n everythin' else, that is."

"Is something wrong, Emily?" Beth came over and took her by the arm.

This would have been the time to tell her of the man following them, but Squinty sauntered over. He pushed his hat back. His bare pate glistened in the morning sun, and it wasn't even hot yet.

"We can stand around jawin' all day or we can drive. I vote that we get on the road."

"Go on," Emily said. "I won't be too far ahead."

Beth looked at her as if she had lost her mind. For all Emily knew, she might have gone around the bend. She was better suited to daylong poker games than jumping at every shadow and movement half-seen out of the corner of her eye. Having a walleye like Squinty would come in handy right now.

Beth climbed into the driver's box. Squinty wasted no time snapping the reins and getting the heavily laden wagon rolling. The wheels cut down into the soft earth, then found harder ground. He picked up speed. Emily knew they'd be on the hard-packed road into Albuquerque soon enough.

She mounted and rather than trailing behind, cut off at an angle, staying in the sparse bosque along the river. After an hour of wending through the thickets and trees, she came out on a rise looking down over a steep hill and a road going down into Albuquerque. Taking the long route caused her to lag behind the wagon. Emily cut toward the road to make better time. Then she drew rein and stared at a dust cloud a mile downhill.

As the dust settled she saw four men clustered about a fifth one, as if getting instructions. She made sure the rifle at her knee slid free easily. Having it hang up in the scabbard might be deadly. She didn't have to overhear what was being said to know they were plotting something illegal. They had a furtive look about them that said more than overheard words ever could.

Galloping downhill, she saw the one in the middle of the ring point farther on down the road. He wheeled about and trotted away from the four. The riders exchanged handshakes and then turned toward the road.

Emily kept up her breakneck pace. She might be wrong. These might be honest, law-abiding wranglers out to find strays. They pulled their bandannas up to cover their faces. This might protect them from dust. It might also be intended to hide their identities.

She bent low and dragged out her rifle. It took great skill to fire accurately from horseback. Emily had never practiced this but that didn't stop her from triggering a round. It went wide, but it got the men's attention.

They lit out. Emily's horse began to falter. She slowed. Her single shot must have run them off. They had to know she was on their trail now. And she must have been wrong about their intent.

Gunfire from ahead rolled uphill toward her. She knew she might kill her horse pushing it harder. She did it anyway. Her worst fears were realized when she hit a level stretch of road and saw the four men circling the ice wagon. Squinty fired wildly with his six-gun. Now and then a shotgun roared out its bull-throated cry of death. That had to be Beth waving the greener around. But they would run out of ammunition quickly.

Emily looked back at her saddlebags. She had purchased more ammo in town. It did Beth and Squinty no good.

She let out a banshee's cry and began firing at the four road agents. Her horse's uneven gait made any hope of shooting straight a fantasy. All she managed to do was draw the four outlaws' attention. Two continued to bedevil Beth and Squinty. The other two came after her.

She pulled back hard on the reins and brought her horse to a dead stop. This gave her a better chance of aiming and hitting one of the outlaws. Her horse still provided a shaky base, but her lead sang closer to the pair galloping toward her.

She fired and one of the riders tumbled from his horse. Emily let out a cry of triumph. If she'd had to place a bet on that shot, she would have guessed she'd missed by a country mile. A quick tug on the cocking lever and she raised the rifle again. Her finger drew back and the hammer fell on an empty chamber.

"No!" She had to reload.

But another shot echoed. And the second outlaw jerked about. He dropped his six-gun and slumped over to cling to his horse's neck with both arms. A second shot blasted him from the saddle. The owlhoot hit the ground hard and kicked up a small dust cloud.

The other two road agents continued to fire at the wagon. Emily saw that Beth had come up dry. Her shotgun fell ominously silent. And then Squinty stopped firing. He had run out of ammunition, too, leaving them at the outlaws' mercy.

Emily fumbled to reload her rifle. By the time she had slipped six more cartridges into the magazine, the pair attacking the wagon called it quits. She got off a single shot at the back of one fleeing road agent, then lowered her weapon.

The wagon was nowhere to be seen, but something else occupied her thoughts. Neither Beth nor Squinty had taken down two of the outlaws. She looked around warily. Because those rounds had found targets in men attacking her didn't mean the shooter was on her side. There might have been a falling out among the road agents. Four had gone after the wagon, but she was certain she had witnessed five before the attack.

Coming from hiding, a single rider approached. She recognized the horse before she did the rider.

"Barleycorn," she said, making it into a curse.

Frank Landry stopped a dozen yards away, his hands high in the air as if surrendering. His rifle was secured in the saddle scabbard and his Colt Navy was securely tucked into his cross-draw holster.

"Fancy meeting you out here," Frank said.

She cursed some more, then said, "Did you shoot your own partners?"

"Them?" Frank Landry glanced over his shoulder and shook his head. "Never saw them before."

"Why'd you kill them?"

She thought he was actually confused at the question. He opened his mouth to respond, then clamped it shut. It took Frank Landry a second to gather his thoughts and answer.

"I made a promise to myself this morning to gun down the first owlhoots I came across. Two got away. I'll bet you dollars to dimes they didn't ride very far."

"Were you supposed to meet them? Where's your rendezvous?"

"Darling, you have the wrong idea entirely. I just saved you from getting that lovely hide of yours punctuated by a dozen bullets."

"What are you doing here?"

She fumed when Frank grinned. He mocked her.

"This assignment sounded like too much for you to finish on your own. I thought I'd give you a hand."

"What are you talking about?"

"Please, Emily, eating all that trail dust hasn't erased your memory. The Society of Buckhorn and Bison? You remember Legende?"

"He sent you?"

"It's not that he thought you'd fail. It's just that I knew how much you needed help." Frank grinned his annoying grin from ear to ear. "I have to admit you've got me bamboozled on how you intend to find Jaime Ochoa's killer by escorting a wagon load of ice to Tombstone."

"Where are the two that hightailed it?" She crammed as many cartridges into the Winchester's magazine as it'd take.

"You admit you need my help?"

"You—" She bit off her curse. Twisting about, she trotted after the two surviving road agents. It came as no surprise when Frank joined her.

"Their boss might be waiting for them, but since they failed to steal all that ice."

"Their boss? Who's that?" She faced Frank squarely. His bright blue eyes shone with humor. He teased her.

"I only caught a glimpse of him, but it might be that I recognized him. Do you think he's the one who killed the banker man?"

"You know him? It figures. Birds of a feather flock together."

"Now, now, my dear, *I* don't count him as one of my associates. Rather, he's more comfortable in *your* social circle. The last time I ran into Dandy Dan Dinkins was in a Larimer Square ginmill. He was busy losing a pile of money to Claude McCrory."

"Slick? The man was *losing* to Slick McCrory?" Emily snorted in contempt. "Nobody loses to him. Slick is about the worst poker player this side of the Big River."

"You don't know him? Dan Dinkins?"

Emily struggled to remember the name and put a face to it. If Frank was right, and damn him, he usually was, he had identified the culprit who had tried to kill her and probably had gunned down Jaime Ochoa.

"What's he want with the ice?" she asked.

Frank shook his head.

"So you don't know everything, do you?"

"I do know we've almost overridden the two that got away," Frank said. He reached for his Colt Navy.

Emily slowed and finally came to a complete halt. They had ridden past the sparse cottonwood stand and into a rocky, arroyo-cut stretch of desert. The tracks they followed disappeared over a sandy rise. If the road agents had kept riding, they traveled along the bottom of an arroyo.

"Ambush," Frank said softly. "That's what I'd do if I had two determined members of the Society after me."

Emily imagined them going over the ridge, silhouetted against the bright, cloudless blue New Mexico sky. They'd be sitting ducks.

"That way," she said. "We skirt the sand dune, get into the arroyo and then run them down while they're waiting to ambush us."

"Not a bad plan," Frank said. "Let's split up. You come at them from the north, I'll hit them from the south. Caught in a crossfire, they won't have a chance."

Emily felt like arguing, but fear of letting the road agents get away drove her to silently acquiesce to Frank's plan. Moreover, it was a good one, but she wasn't going to admit that. He had trumped her repeatedly, saving her from the other two road agents, then identifying the killer of the bank president.

She galloped hard, found a saddle between two dunes, then cut due west. The arroyo opened in front of her. She bent low and let her horse leap over the bank and hit hard in the middle of the gravel-strewn gully. It was still too early in the season for runoff from the high mountains to fill the dried water channel from bank to bank.

Emily got control of her horse and turned southward just as gunfire sounded.

She rode hard and saw one of the outlaws firing wildly in the direction where Frank approached on foot. She took careful aim and fired. The road agent took a single step forward and fell facedown.

The intense silence that settled on the arroyo hurt her ears.

"You all right?" Frank's call broke the quiet.

"Are you? I shot a man in the back to keep him from killing you."

Frank Landry sauntered up and kicked at the outlaw she had shot.

"You've either been practicing or you got lucky. Good shot."

"Is either one of them Dandy Dan Dinkins?"

She slid from the saddle and walked to where Frank searched the dead outlaw.

"You'd know him by the way he dresses. He's a real clothes horse."

"Not unlike other people I know," she said. "Do you still spend more on velvet coats with silk lapels and paisley vests than I do on fancy gowns?"

"I've got the money. Too bad you sound like you're on a losing streak. Don't try bluffing as much and maybe you'll win more hands."

"I was raking in the pots when Legende sent me the telegram putting me onto this assignment."

"Neither of 'em is Dandy Dan. That must mean ..."

Emily locked eyes with her ex-husband. They both came to the same conclusion. If Dandy Dan Dinkins wasn't with the gang that tried to steal the ice, that meant he was ... stealing the ice.

18

"You boys are gonna get rich," Dandy Dan Dinkins said in a booming, confident voice. He looked around at the four men astride their horses. He stood in the middle, studying them. What he saw he liked. Greed etched each and every face.

Perfect.

"You ain't comin' with us?" The tall, scrawny one Dinkins pegged as the leader spoke for the others. Their heads all bobbed up and down like a chicken finding seed grain in the poultry yard.

"There's a marshal with a couple deputies nearby. I'll decoy them away while you hit the wagon." Dinkins saw that this satisfied them. They wanted to hear how easy the robbery was going to be.

"You sure this here wagon's loaded with gold?"

"Not gold," Dinkins said, improvising. "Silver. Coins. They're carrying bags of silver cartwheels for the Railroad Bank in Albuquerque. The president has been having his shipments from Santa Fe stolen, so he decided to sneak a half dozen sacks of coins into town using an unmarked wagon without a platoon of guards that'd only draw attention. I don't know how much you'll get, but it'll be a bag of silver for each of you."

"I never heard of this here Railroad Bank," the leader said, drawling as the thought worked its way to the top of his brain.

"Why do you think they're moving so much silver secretly? It's a brand spanking new bank. They need all that silver to set up business. They won't open until they get plenty of money to stack in their new steel vault brought out from St. Louis all special." Dinkins warmed to the tall tale, then bit off any further elaboration. Men telling the truth seldom embellished the facts the way he was.

And there wasn't a bare naked fact anywhere in what he said. Any fear he'd oversold the robbery disappeared in a flash.

"What if there's more than you promised?" The leader spat a gob of tobacco and wiped his mouth with his sleeve. "You layin' claim to that?"

Dinkins knew in any con it was best to keep the mark's thoughts on how much money they'd make and avoid any details that would reveal the hoax. Dinkins was ready to feed the greed.

"Yes, sir, I am. I trust you not to divvy up extra bags and stuff your own until the seams pop." Dinkins knew they expected to hear this. If he hadn't demanded something from the robbery they'd get mighty suspicious. All he had to do was keep avarice foremost in their minds so any common sense was pushed aside.

"Where do we meet up after we relieve them of their extry silver?"

Dinkins hadn't considered this when he concocted his web of lies. He looked around, then said in a low voice, "You know the territory better 'n I do. Where would you suggest?"

"The White Elephant in town's a good place. We kin drift in one or two at a time. Nobody'd notice us that way. The saloon's down the street from the railroad station, so they get plenny of customers waitin' to catch a train."

Dinkins had never been to Albuquerque and hoped he'd be able to avoid it now. Rumor had it that the law was quick on the draw and the marshal spent a fair amount of time pawing through wanted posters. While his face wasn't likely to be on any dodger, taking a chance he wouldn't be recognized was foolhardy.

"You boys are real good at plotting and planning," he said insincerely. They failed to catch the sarcasm in his tone. Greed still ruled their hearts and heads.

"Let's get to it," the leader said. "The sooner we're ridin' away after ransackin' that wagon, the sooner we'll be rich."

"My mouth's drier than a desert sand dune," Dinkins said. "Go get 'em so we can meet at that saloon for a victory drink!"

With a loud whoop, the four wheeled about and galloped toward the road. Dinkins estimated they'd overtake the wagon in about twenty minutes. That gave him time to meet the marshal and any deputies he'd brought with him.

He took his time reaching the small town outside Albuquerque. From the look of Tres Pasos the law needed all the money they could scare up. Just riding close to the town was enough to send gossip rippling the length of the short main street. By the time his boots hit the ground, the marshal was already standing behind him.

"Something I can do for you, young fella?" The gray-bearded lawman took off his hat and wiped sweat from his brown-skinned dome. The shine of sun off his bald pate made Dinkins squint.

"You're just the man I want to see, Marshal."

"Now that's not what I usually hear. You must have quite a tale to tell."

"Nothing all that unusual, I'm afraid. I was out on the trail, down by the Rio Grande, and happened to overhear four gents talking like they intended to hold up a freight wagon making its way south."

"Do tell. What's your concern? You know the wagon driver?"

"Nothing of the sort. I got the feeling they intended to kill the driver and everyone riding along. That's not the sort of thing I cotton to." Dinkins faked a tiny shudder. "Makes my blood run cold hearing about such a dastardly crime."

"What's in the wagon? Something real valuable?"

Dinkins heard the greed in the law dog's voice.

"Whoever ventures along the Jornado del Muerto has got to be carrying something valuable. Don't you see that, Marshal?"

"There's not a lot of traffic yjtpihj Tres Pasos even though we're not more 'n five miles from the road. We're mostly here to supply pinto bean farmers or them folks raisin' alfalfa. There's not even a decent ranch within fifty miles of here. Just farmers sucking water out of the Rio Grande using acequias." The marshal sounded bitter about that.

"It's a shame, then, that there's not much in the way of decent beef to be had," Dinkins said.

"There's that," the marshal said. He settled his hat squarely on his head, pulling both sides down over the tops of his jug ears. "What is it you want from me?"

"I admit I could have been mistaken about the four travelers' intentions, but I don't think so. You may save some lives if you check on that wagon." Dinkins shrugged. "There's some kind of travel fee in these parts, isn't there? Collect that for your trouble if nothing's wrong. And if there is, why, four desperadoes like them must have rewards on their heads. You could be four or five hundred dollars to the good."

The mention of money lit up the man's lined face. Dinkins never knew solid mahogany could smile.

"Down by the river, you say? That's out of my jurisdiction. Just a little."

"Just a little, but not that much," Dinkins said, helping him find a reason to stop the ice wagon.

"Why don't you ride along with me to help identify the miscreants?"

"Miscreants," Dinkins repeated. "Now that's a fine word to describe those four. Miscreants." Dinkins chuckled at the lawman's expression of approval.

"Let me get my deputy, and we'll run those owlhoots down."

"Those miscreant owlhoots," Dinkins corrected.

He blinked when the marshal ducked into the tiny jailhouse and came back out with a long-barreled greener. The lawman held it up and said, "This here's the best deputy I ever had. He's quiet, don't give me no lip and is reliable. Better 'n all that, I don't have to pay him nothing, either."

"Just feed him a few shells when he gets hungry," Dinkins said. He stepped up and waited for the marshal to round the building. He returned in a couple minutes astride a swayback nag that walked as if every step was its last.

"This ole mare's got a few miles on her," the marshal allowed. "She's got a few more left, too."

Dinkins and the marshal walked from town. They reached the river fifteen minutes later. Deep wagon ruts in the soft earth showed where the ice wagon had rolled through recently.

"This is the trail. I'm not much of a tracker, but you'd have to be blind not to—" Dinkins cut off his words when gunfire came from a ways down the river.

"Sounds as if a spirited battle is being waged," the marshal said. He put his heels to his mare. To Dinkins' surprise the old nag showed considerable speed. Even if he hadn't intended to hang back, keeping up with the galloping marshal would have been difficult.

He worked his way to drier, firmer ground. By the time the marshal's shotgun blared, the pistol and rifle fire was over and done. Dinkins approached slowly. He expected his four dupes to be dead. Or if they had gunned down the driver and Beth Randall and the annoying redhead riding with them, the freighters would be in bad shape.

It took him a few seconds to size up the situation. The marshal stood over the driver, shotgun pointed at him. There wasn't a trace of any of the others duped into being road agents. Dinkins rode closer.

"This one claims to be the wagon driver. I don't like his looks."

"You've got a real talent for being a lawman," Dinkins said. "That's one of the four men I overheard plotting to steal the wagon."

"Whatcha goin' on about? I ain't stealin' the wagon. I work for Miz Randall. I'm drivin' fer her!"

"Where is she?" Dinkins cut in before the marshal got his wits about him. It was obvious the driver, squint and all, belonged with the wagon. He wasn't even packing a sidearm. "I don't see anyone here but you."

"And we heard gunshots," the marshal chimed in. Getting cut out of asking the questions rankled him.

"We was jumped. There was four of 'em!" Squinty Houseman tried to sit up. The marshal prodded him back flat on the ground. "Miz Randall and them other two held them off. Miz O'Connor's more of a gun slick than she looks. My piece is up in the driver's box."

Dinkins considered what the driver said. Someone else

rode with the wagon and was adept enough at slinging lead to chase off four men intent on robbery. Who that was hardly mattered. Everything was coming together for him. All he needed was a lucky break.

"That sounds suspicious, Marshal," he said. "This one's left behind?"

"They all took after the road agents. Just you wait. They'll be back and tell you I'm their driver." Houseman tried to sit up again and, once more, the lawman wasn't having any of it.

"What are you hauling?" asked the marshal. He stepped back, but he kept a sharp eye on the supine man. Using the muzzle of his shotgun, he lifted back the rear canvas flap. From his frown he had no idea what weighed down the wagon so much.

"Why's it so cold in there?" the marshal asked.

"Ice. We got a ton of ice as cargo." The driver sat up. When the marshal didn't order him back down, he stood.

"This sounds like a story you need to hear in full, Marshal," Dinkins said. "Take him on back to town. Keep him locked up and see if those people he's going on about show up. If they don't then you know he's one of the gang and they left him behind."

"What about the wagon?" The marshal shook his head. "He's telling the truth about there being nothing but ice back there. At least that's the way it looks to me."

"Take him back to Tres Pasos, and I'll watch the wagon."

"This is Miz Randall's! You can't—" The driver let out a yelp when the marshal swung his shotgun around and landed the barrel alongside Squinty's temple.

"You've got the right idea. I'll get to the bottom of this. And if his lady friend shows up, she can pay the portage fee."

"What's that?" the driver asked, rubbing his temple.

"That tells it all, Marshal," Dinkins said. "No portage fee's been paid."

"Will you be all right by your lonesome?"

"I'll keep an eye peeled for any trouble."

"I wish there were more citizens like you, mister." The marshal gestured with his shotgun for the driver to unfasten the right lead mule and mount, bareback. "You don't need to bring the wagon around. Missing a flea-bitten mule makes pulling the wagon a chore." He looked at the deep ruts caused by the ponderous weight and shook his head. Dinkins heard him mutter, "Ice?" and then get the driver trotting ahead of him.

Dandy Dan Dinkins waited for them to disappear in the direction of the town. He looked around for Pete Randall's wife and whoever she had lending her a hand. For all he could tell, he was alone on the bank of the river.

He hopped over to the driver's box, secured his horse's reins, then got the five-mule team pulling. It was a good thing he didn't intend going far. He wanted to be away from where he might be found quickly. It took close to half an hour to hit a rocky patch that wouldn't betray his tracks.

Then he pulled over to examine the ice blocks. Pete Randall had to be frozen in one. And with him a map to where the bank loot was stashed. For the first time since the bank robbery, Dandy Dan Dinkins felt that he was going to be very, very rich very, very soon.

19

"We've been decoyed away," Emily O'Connor said in disgust. "Squinty should have been here with the wagon." She swallowed hard. "And Beth is missing."

Frank Landry wandered about, studying the tracks. He shook his head slowly, struggling to make sense of what had happened.

"Two of the gang trying to steal the wagon are pushing up daisies," he said. Then he smiled without humor. "They'd be pushing up daisies if we'd buried them. Coyote food," he said. "Unless the buzzards get them first."

"And you let two more escape," Emily said.

Frank looked at her in surprise.

"*I* let them get away? I saved you from getting murdered by them."

"So where's Beth? Where is the wagon? Maybe Squinty drove on with it into Albuquerque to keep it safe."

"You don't sound as if you believe that. Your driver's a little on the crooked side, isn't he?"

"He's not my choice for a dedicated hired hand. He worked for the Randalls, and they trusted him."

"You don't sound as if you believe that, either." Frank walked in a circle. "The wagon was driven due west but one of the team is missing. Two riders came here, two left. But one of them rode off with a mule from your team."

"That doesn't make any sense."

"Carrying a load of ice doesn't make much sense, unless you like cold beer," he said. Frank continued to spiral outward from where the wagon had been parked. He reached for his Colt Navy slung in his cross-draw holster when vegetation ahead of him shivered.

There wasn't much wind blowing. A rabbit would have hightailed it a long time ago with so much human activity around the river. A predator—other than a human—wouldn't find anything interesting here. He cocked his pistol and motioned for Emily to stay put.

He cursed under his breath when she came up, her rifle pointed more at him than the bush.

"Come on out. I've got you covered." Frank was tempted to fire a warning shot, but with Emily so close waving her rifle around, that might frighten her. Her bullet would take him out, not someone hiding. He wondered if she'd be the least bit stricken over such an accidental shooting.

"Yeah, you get your scrawny butt out where we can see you!" Emily was flushed and she was keyed up, ready for another fight.

No response. The bush shivered a tad more. Frank waited, but Emily pushed past him and poked her rifle into the clump of vegetation.

A moan sounded. Emily pushed the greenery aside with her rifle while Frank aimed straight for the revealed person.

"Beth!" Emily dropped her rifle and grabbed her friend,

pulling her out of the bush. She glared at Frank. "Put that away. You're scaring her!"

"She fainted," Frank said as he holstered his six-shooter. He stepped over the rifle Emily had dropped and helped his ex-wife drag the unconscious woman clear of the bush.

"She hasn't fainted," Emily said sharply. "See?"

Frank shrugged. Beth Randall had a knot on her head the size of a hen's egg. She had taken cover in the vegetation and tripped, hitting her head on a rock.

"Emily! They're attacking. Stop them!" Beth came awake with a start, clutched at Emily and pulled her close.

"There, there. It's all right. I ran them off."

"We ran them off," Frank said. "Two of them are still on the loose, but I don't think they'll be back." He had returned his six-gun to his holster but rested his hand on the butt of his Colt. The firefight with the outlaws had been brief but intense. They had swooped down, obviously not expecting him to be riding along behind the wagon.

When they opened fire, Emily had shot back. Frank had caught them in a crossfire. It took only seconds for the surviving pair to run for the high country.

"Where's Squinty?" Beth pushed past Emily and stood, looking around. "And the wagon?"

"We aren't sure," Emily said. "Frank thinks someone rode off with Squinty. It looks to me as if he drove the wagon away from the river."

"To save the cargo?" Beth held her head in both hands and moaned. "Find him. You've got to find him. We've got to! And the ice!"

"There are a couple things we can do, but you don't have a horse." Frank saw the woman regained her senses but still hadn't thought things through.

"She can ride with me," Emily said. She glared at him, daring him to say otherwise.

"Go after the two riders, then. I don't think they're the outlaws who survived. I'll track the wagon. If this Squinty fellow drove it off as you think, he'll need help. The outlaws will be after him if they are serious about holding you up."

"Because the two remaining road agents might go after him," Emily said, more to Beth than to agree with him. He might as well have been talking to the wind.

Frank's mind raced as he tried to make sense of the tracks. Four riders left the area, along with the wagon. He knew two sets of tracks belonged to the outlaws. Sending Emily and Beth after the other pair was foolhardy. It'd be better if they sought out the wagon, if the Randall's hired hand was driving.

In his gut, Frank thought someone else drove the wagon. But who? There were too many conflicting riders leaving tracks.

"We've got to hurry," Beth said. "If anyone opens the crates, the ice will melt."

Frank wanted to know more about the wisdom of shipping a wagon creaking with ice, but this wasn't the right time to ask.

Emily steered Beth toward her horse but hung back to speak with Frank.

"You're sure that the outlaws went after the wagon? And that the other tracks belong to someone else?"

"I saw a signpost on the road a mile or two back. Those tracks seem to lead in the general direction of the town. The riders might be from there. And even if they aren't, get to the town and call out the marshal."

"What? The magnificent Frank Landry can't handle a couple road agents on his own?" Her needling tone riled him a mite, but he had developed a thick skin to her criticism over the years they were married. Emily didn't mean much by it. She was Boston Irish and fiery by nature.

"You mean Squinty needs my help, if he's with the wagon.

Only five mules are pulling it, so he can't have gotten too far with a lopsided team." He held back his suspicion that someone else drove away with the cargo.

For a moment, Emily looked at him and he saw concern in her bright green eyes. Then she whirled away, gathered Beth and mounted. They rode away at a trot, leaving Frank in the midst of the confounding tracks.

The only way to settle matters was to find the wagon. He swung into the saddle and headed away from the river, the deep tracks leading him to higher ground. A moment of satisfaction warmed him when he spotted the wagon's tall canvas covering within ten minutes. He slipped the leather thong off the Colt's hammer and got ready to shoot it out again.

Before, he knew he faced four men. He had ridden up on them from the rear and taken them by surprise. Now he had no idea what lay ahead.

He swung his leg over the saddle and dropped to the ground. Advancing on foot gave him a better chance to repeat the surprise. Moving slowly, he approached from the rear. The tailgate had been lowered. Three blocks of ice had been removed. Frank Landry listened hard and heard the team braying and pawing at the ground. The wagon tracks showed the team had pulled the wagon farther from where the three missing blocks had hit the ground.

Frank edged around and immediately saw two of the crates holding the ice. The third one was nowhere to be seen. He looked into the driver's box. A sawed-off shotgun was held by a leather strap near where Squinty would sit. Since the weapon was in place and the man's six-gun and belt lay on the floor of the driver's box, that meant Squinty wasn't armed.

Cautiously going along the team, he caught up the traces and saw that the right lead mule had been unharnessed. Somewhere in the back of his mind he had entertained the notion that the leather had frayed or been cut and the mule had escaped on its own. Whoever had the mule had taken it intentionally.

Using a few large rocks to hold down the trailing harness, Frank wanted to keep the mules from racing off if gunplay started. He carefully rounded the team and went to the ice blocks. The wood frames had been broken open, but that was the only obvious damage.

The wagon had come up an incline. He found skid marks where the third block of ice had slid downhill. Frank caught his breath as methodical hammering sounds reached him. He slipped down and followed a contour leading to an arroyo that, during the height of spring runoff, fed the Rio Grande. Now it was almost dry other than a thin trickle down the middle.

Crouched on the far side of the third crate, a man used a rock to chip away at the ice. Most of the wood frame had been broken into splinters and peeled away already.

Frank drew his pistol. Something warned the man so industriously pounding at the ice. He looked up, startled. He ducked down behind the ice block, and Frank knew he had trouble brewing.

Frank fired and immediately dived for cover as return fire filled the air around him. He had shot once. The outlaw working on the ice emptied his six-gun.

"Give up," Frank called. "I've got you dead to rights!"

The road agent replied with another leaden barrage. This forced Frank to hunt for better cover. The few drought-stunted shrubs and rocks poking up out of the hillside were nowhere near enough to protect him from such deadly fire. He had thought his enemy had only a single six-shooter. To fire again so rapidly meant he had a second six-gun.

Frank thanked his lucky stars that he hadn't tried rushing the thief when he thought he'd come up empty with the first pistol.

He chanced a quick look up. For some reason the road agent wasn't targeting him. Then he saw why. Emily had blundered onto the fight. All the bullets sang in her direction—and it was a wild song of death.

She had fallen to the ground into a shallow depression. There wasn't any way she dared stir. If the road agent ever got the range she was a goner.

His initial thought had been to rush the man firing so accurately. That would have ended up getting a gut filled with lead. But Frank saw no way for Emily to get away unless the gunman was distracted. Standing up, he yelled and fired a couple times to draw attention away from the redhead.

All he got was a round that sent his hat flying. He flinched involuntarily. His distraction hadn't been enough to give Emily a chance to run for better cover.

"He's hiding behind the block of ice," Frank shouted.

"I can see that. I've got eyes," Emily snapped back. "Can't you shoot the ice and shatter it?"

"He's got a couple more blocks to hide behind, even if I could. And I can't."

"Thanks for letting him know," Emily called sarcastically. "Why not just up and surrender?"

Frank held down his ire at the woman. They were both in a dire position. More bullets whined in his direction, then returned to bedeviling Emily.

"What do you want? The ice? Take it," Frank shouted. No response.

He tried wiggling away and was forced back by well-aimed bullets.

"What do you want?" Frank called. "We'll give it to you."

"I want you to die!" The fierce answer wasn't what Frank had expected. He had no reason to save the ice, not if it meant getting away from such a deadly ambush.

"Keep the ice. Let us go," Frank said, hunting for a better

hiding place. He winced as a bullet tore past his left shoulder and cut through the hitherto untouched sleeve. No amount of patching would restore his fine coat. For that the outlaw was going to pay!

"No!" Emily's aggrieved cry distracted him. "That's not yours. Ride on out and we'll let you go, no matter what you've done."

Frank considered the fiery redhead's words. She must know something he didn't. She offered exoneration for—what? Chances were good the gunman they faced had something to do with the Taos robbery. If so, that meant this was the killer Allister Legende wanted brought to justice.

"You think two more deaths will make it hard for me to get a good night's sleep?" The hidden man laughed.

Frank took a shot and missed. His bullet chipped off a corner of the block of ice where the outlaw crouched. By now the ice was beginning to melt and dirt from the hillside turned it into a muddy coffin-shaped mess.

"Both of us rush him at the same time," Frank called to Emily. He hoped she didn't think this was a good idea. He didn't. All he wanted was to distract the gunman enough for one or the other of them to get a decent shot at him.

As he feared, the tactic failed. Emily stayed put and exposing himself only drew more fire. The outlaw had a perfect spot to shoot at them. Pinned down, all they could hope for was that the block of ice melted away. Even then the road agent had two more to hide behind.

"Now!"

A storm of bullets filled the air. Frank blinked. He had no idea how Emily fired so fast with her rifle. He became more confused when she called to him, "I'm out of bullets."

The air filled with even more deadly lead. All of it flew toward the ice and drove the desperado from hiding. Frank swung up to his knees and got off a few more shots. His six-gun came up empty without hitting anything.

"This the varmint?"

Frank looked over his shoulder at a mounted man with a shotgun trained on him.

"Naw, he ain't the one. And that's Miz Randall's friend, Miz O'Connor."

Behind the scattergun-toting rider on a mule obviously taken from the wagon's team sat a dilapidated wreck of a man with one eye screwed tightly shut.

"Squinty! You bought the law!" Emily went to them and looked up. "You must be the marshal from that town we passed a while back."

Frank caught the glint of light off the lawman's badge. Although he worked with the law more than not these days, thanks to the Society of Buckhorn and Bison, he locked horns with the officials over his profession as whiskey peddler and ... now and again the "almost legal" chores he did for Legende.

"You surely did pull our fat from the fire, Marshal," he said.

The lawman grunted, said something about getting back to town, wheeled around and left the three of them on the hillside.

"It doesn't look like he's much interested in running to ground our attacker," Frank said.

"And thief. That man stole the wagon and the ice," Emily said angrily.

Frank pursed his lips. What the fiery woman said was true. And it hardly made any sense. The owlhoot was willing to leave their dead bodies under the New Mexico sun. For what? A few hundred pounds of ice? That he tried to chip away in a dry arroyo?

20

Frank Landry swiped at the flood of sweat on his forehead. He stepped back and started to wipe his hands off on his trousers, then thought better of it. He was dusty and dirty. Getting rid of the grime from loading the blocks of ice back into the freight wagon only took another step toward ruining his fine clothing. He had spent a fortune on the trousers and coat to impress his clients.

He glanced toward Emily O'Connor. And the ladies, he mentally added. He always wanted to appear at his best, no matter what he was selling. But now he might as well throw himself into the Rio Grande, wash off the dirt and then dry himself in the wan sun of late winter.

"Early spring," he said to himself.

"That's all that's kept the ice from melting," Beth Randall said. She used a handkerchief to wipe sweat from her face. She hefted a hammer and looked at her handiwork. The block of ice the road agent had exposed and tried to chip away at once more rested snugly in its wood coffin. The ice had melted enough to turn the dirt on the surface to mud, but Frank doubted anyone buying the ice cared much.

He went to the block and tried to clean off the mud, because such filth annoyed him. Several swipes got him nowhere. The dirt had become a part of the surface still exposed.

"What was he after?" He looked around, almost expecting the road agent to pop up with an explanation.

"Could you go pull some of those weeds?" Emily pointed to feathery greenery. "We can use that to replace the sawdust insulation lost when the blocks of ice slid from the wagon."

Frank started toward the ankle-high weeds, then stopped. Squinty was already obeying. Frank grumbled to himself that he wasn't a hired hand waiting hand and foot on Emily. They weren't married and being at her beck and call wasn't getting him anywhere.

Wherever that might be.

Legende wanted Jaime Ochoa's killer caught. Emily had been given the assignment but Frank wanted to show her up. It was that simple. If he had a lick of sense he'd get on Barleycorn and head back to Taos. Getting Buck Isaacson's still fired up meant supplying the entire territory with moonshine so profitable he could buy Mudflats Distilling and control a sizable percentage of all liquor sales west of the Mississippi. If he took a notion, starting up a tequila distillery might even be worthwhile. The señoritas down Mexico way would be a real incentive for him.

"Frank. Frank!"

He jumped.

"You're lost in one of your wild flights of fancy, aren't you?" Emily glared at him.

"You make it sound wrong." He felt a little sheepish. She was always the more practical one. It had something to do with the way she played cards like a machine, dealing and shoving out just the right number of chips after cutting all kinds of mental didos.

"Squinty and Beth can get back on the road," Emily said. "We can track down the varmint and make him tell us what he wants from Beth."

"There're two others. He had something to do with them trying to pirate your friend's cargo."

"Hmm, I suppose so. The four attacked when they did with the fifth man waiting to swoop in. That sounds like he planned it. Or one of them did."

"It was the fancy dressed galoot," Squinty said. "When I was ridin' back to town with the marshal, he said the one that tried to steal the ice tole him 'bout the other four."

"Dinkins turned on his own gang? That doesn't make any sense," Emily said.

"It does, if he never expected them to be successful. They get killed or run off, the marshal arrests whoever's on the wagon—in this case it was Squinty—and that leaves the wagon unprotected so he can steal the ice. I'd say it worked pretty well." Frank had to hand it to Dandy Dan. He risked very little. If anyone got shot up or arrested, it'd be the other four. As soon as Beth and everyone riding with the wagon were removed, he had a clear path to thievery.

"The only thing that stopped him was me," Frank said. "Dinkins didn't count on there being an extra six-gun in the fight."

"You have a point, Mr. Landry " Beth pulled herself up into the driver's box next to Squinty. "While I'd rest easy knowing you'd brought him to justice, please don't go after him. Guarding the cargo makes me feel much safer." She smiled winningly. Frank melted like ice in the sun.

"I'll stay with the wagon, Beth," Emily cut in. "Mr. Landry is just itching to run that scoundrel to ground, aren't you, Frank?"

"Dinkins iss responsible for planning everything and wasn't just along for the ride. I'll find him," Frank said. "You

185

stay with the wagon." He directed the order at Emily, who bristled. He couldn't help himself when he added, "I'll see that Jaime Ochoa's death is avenged, just as Legende wants." For a moment he thought she was going to demand to ride along. Then she sagged just a little, and he knew he had her.

Any glory in bringing the outlaw responsible for a long litany of crimes to justice would be his and his alone.

"Catch up with us and let me know the details so I can report to the Society," Emily said. She gave him an insincere smile, mounted and blazed a trail back to the main road, Squinty and Beth following her lead.

Frank felt suddenly alone. He patted his gelding's neck and said, "It's just you and me again, Barleycorn. We'll show her. Them."

He mounted and began his hunt for the outlaw's tracks.

"I'll grant you this much. You're one determined cuss," Frank Landry said, looking up from the tracks.

He expected the outlaw to light out for parts unknown but was surprised when the road agent's trail paralleled the road along the river. He wasn't giving up. If anything, from the looks of the spoor, he intended to hold up the freight wagon again.

Frank shook his head in wonder. What was so all fired important about the ice? If the dandy he tracked meant to ruin the Randalls, all he had to do was destroy the wagon. Let the blocks melt. The water would be sucked into the dry desert almost instantly.

Images of Dandy Dan Dinkins using a rock to chip away at the one hunk of ice kept taunting Frank. There was something going on that he couldn't understand.

The sun was almost gone behind distant mountains on

the far horizon. He shivered as he pulled his coat collar up to protect his neck and cheeks.

"So Squinty claimed that the marshal thinks Dinkins dresses better 'n me?" Frank snorted. That made it all the more important to stop the outlaw. It was one thing to steal the ice. Maybe he had also killed the bank president and stolen the loot from the robbery. But being considered a Beau Brummel to the point that someone like Frank Landry in all his finery was ignored? An absolute insult!

He walked his horse along until the tracks began vanishing in gathering shadow. Finally twilight cloaked the land so much that he lost the trail. Unless he lit a torch and tried to track that way, he was done for the night. Frank hunted for a decent spot to camp. He was a ways from the river, but occasional feeder streams ran down to the Rio Grande. He had plenty of water.

But he wanted a sheltered spot. The night wind kicked up with the icy knife edges of winter still slashing away at his exposed face and hands. If he lit a fire, he didn't want the road agent to spot him.

He considered pressing on. He knew the direction of travel necessary to overtake Dinkins. If the outlaw had no idea anyone was after him, he'd light a fire. That would give Frank the upper hand.

"Rest or press on?" he asked Barleycorn. "I'm bone tired from working to get the ice loaded again, but the trail's been easy enough. It's just been long and I haven't had much to eat. Why, I—"

A shadow to his left shifted a few inches. Frank launched himself from horseback and landed hard on the sunbaked ground. A bullet sang its deadly song through the space where his head had bobbed along an instant before. He rolled over and clawed out his Colt Navy. The man he hunted had the same idea that he did.

Dinkins knew he was being tracked.

Frank came around and found a clump of prickly pears to hide behind. The soft-padded cacti provided no shield at all from a bullet, but he was able to hide. Make the outlaw waste his ammo. If Dinkins fired enough, his pistol flash would pinpoint him in the dark.

Frank stretched flat as juicy pieces of prickly pear exploded above him. Getting the sticky sap off his clothing would be a chore.

It'd only be a chore if he stayed alive.

Frank moved to a spot where he peered through the now torn-up cactus. A thick-trunked, towering cottonwood tree a few yards away gave shelter to his attacker. He cocked his pistol, rested the butt on the ground and waited. When the shadows moved again, he fired.

"Give up. You don't have a chance," Frank shouted. He felt confident that he had winged his adversary. He remained prone, waiting patiently.

A minute went by. Then two. A lucky shot might have taken down the outlaw. But Frank had learned not to rely on luck. If it turned bad in a situation like this, he'd be buzzard bait. A third minute passed. He felt the pressure of time. Barleycorn had run off, stranding him. If he lost his horse, he'd be on foot for a long time.

Five minutes.

When he was sure he'd lain in wait for ten minutes, he came to his knees and peered over the clump of cacti. The twilight had deepened into night. He had no idea when the moon would rise, but when it did, it would be behind him.

Frank climbed to his feet. Moving in a crouch, he advanced, trying to use the contours of the land to his advantage. It worked. He didn't catch an ounce of lead in the gut. He pressed into the cottonwood's trunk. All he heard was the distant rush of the river and, more telling, sounds of a desert come to life. Nocturnal predators sought dinner. Their prey rustled about scrounging for their own meals.

He spun around the tree, ready to fire. Shadows mocked him. Frank dropped to his knees and found boot prints. By now the moon edged above the far horizon over the mountains. The wan silver rays revealed a small black patch in the dirt. He pressed his finger into the muck and rubbed thumb and forefinger together.

"Dried blood," he decided. "But not much. I grazed him and he lit a shuck."

Frank wasn't sure if he felt good that Dinkins refused to carry on the fight and had rushed off or if he wanted the cat and mouse game to be over. Most of all he wanted to find why the outlaw wanted to steal a wagon creaking under the weight of frozen water.

He prowled about until he saw hoofprints heading southward.

"Parallel to the river. He's not giving up. Dinkins is still after the ice in the wagon."

Frank heaved a sigh and slid his six-shooter back into its holster. Then he spent the next half hour hunting for his own horse. Somehow, Barleycorn wasn't eager to have a rider again. Frank Landry understood the feeling. The longer he was on the trail, the more confusing everything became.

21

"Melt, damn you, melt!" Dandy Dan Dinkins hammered away at the block of ice with his pistol butt. Seeing no progress, he holstered his iron and picked up a decent-sized rock with a sharp edge like a stone axe. Blow after blow landed on the block of frozen water but only tiny chips flew off.

He wiped away the dirt that covered the surface. He had lured the man and woman away and the marshal had taken the driver off to town to question him. Dinkins had removed Randall's wife with a decent whack to the head. Driving the team had been tricky since the marshal had confiscated the team's right lead mule for the hired hand to ride back into town.

It took all of Dinkins' concentration but he drove the wagon away from the river road. The man and woman who argued constantly would return when they had either tracked down the pair of outlaws who had survived or gave up in frustration. By the time they got back, Dinkins intended to have the ice broken up.

"You've got it," he said to the ice. "I can see it." He wiped away more dirt. The ice was crystal clear but turning foggy inside as the sunlight worked down into the interior. Pete Randall stared up at him with dead, frozen eyes.

Sticking from the man's vest was a partially torn sheet of paper. Dinkins had seen the rest of the map but it had showed him nothing. When he broke off enough of the ice to take the rest of the map, he'd know where the gold from the bank was hidden.

"All mine," he chortled. "You tried to cheat me, but you ended up as a stiff." He had to laugh at that. Randall was dead and frozen stiff.

And the map was only a foot away.

He continued to hammer away at the ice, but the rock he'd picked up cracked. He hunted for another one made of harder stone.

"This is taking too long. Too damned long," he grunted. He held a new rock in both hands and continued to whale away. Randall might as well have been encased in steel for all the progress he made. After a few minutes of pounding, all he had accomplished was to make the icy surface opaque. He had hoped for a crack to split the block by now, but all he had done was obscure his goal.

The map. He had to get the map from Randall's pocket!

More dirt settled down on the surface, then seemed to bond like plaster. Dinkins didn't have to see his goal. He knew how far he had to knap. But as frantically as he worked, only an inch broke free. Time began to weigh heavily on him. Before long, the man and woman riding with Beth Randall would get on his trail. Hiding the wagon tracks hadn't been possible. He had left the wagon in plain sight at the top of a hill, opened the tailgate and pushed out the blocks one by one after checking to find the coldly imprisoned Pete Randall.

He had been lucky. The third crate held the body and had

slid down the hillside. After such a ride he expected the ice to shatter. Instead, all that had happened was peeling away the sides of the wooden crate. That saved him a few minutes work. He wished the ice had dropped from the sky and broken into a million pieces.

Even pressed against the ice, he began to sweat from exertion. He lifted the rock for yet another swing when he heard a horse approaching. It was on the far side of the hill, on the other side of the wagon. He dropped the rock and drew his six-shooter. Dinkins rested his weapon on the filthy top of the ice block and squeezed off a round.

He fired blind, but the effect was immediate. Return fire. A bullet caused a tiny geyser in front of him. Distracted, he realized he had done the right thing not firing repeatedly at the ice. It hardly chipped.

Dinkins fired until his six-shooter came up empty, then drew his spare. He had tucked it into his belt before stealing the wagon back at the river. As he expected, the man coming after him was the dude who argued constantly with the redhead. Dinkins got off a couple more shots but missed.

He rested his hand on the marred ice. At the rate he had been going, it'd be another hour to free the part of Randall's body with the map. He scooped up dirt and spread it on the surface.

"You'd have to see through solid adobe to know what's inside," he said to himself. He duck-walked away, using the ice to hide his retreat. He wasn't going to shoot it out. He ran low on ammo and the gunfire would attract the fiery-haired woman and probably the marshal, if he was still in the area. There'd be another chance to get the map.

He reached his horse and mounted. No gunfire. The fancy-dressed man thought to wait him out. A careless moment, a quick, accurate shot, and the gunfight would be over.

Dinkins rode slowly away, keeping parallel to the river. He knew where they headed. He'd lay a trap for them somewhere farther south.

He rode steadily until twilight. He ached all over and his mood had turned increasingly foul. Finding a decent spot to make camp, he tethered his horse behind a cottonwood tree and began laying a fire. Just as he started to put a lucifer to it, he stopped. The night sounds had stopped.

He wasn't alone.

Dinkins gathered his gear and retreated behind the tree. Cursing under his breath, he saddled his horse and secured his gear. As he finished he heard movement on the far side of where he'd started to pitch camp. Bracing his gun hand against the tree, he peered into the gloom. Nothing showed.

Then he caught a hint of a man moving up from the direction of the river. The moon has risen just a little, casting its pale light on the landscape. Dinkins fired.

And he immediately regretted it. The return fire homed in on his muzzle flash. A sudden burning streak across his side caused him to recoil. He sat heavily, momentarily stunned. Then he probed his left hip. His fingers came away wet with sticky blood. He turned slightly and let the wound leak onto the ground to keep from soaking into his coat more than it already had.

Dinkins remembered the waiting game that they had played back where he attacked the ice block. Exhausted, needing to tend his wound, he edged away and pulled himself up into his saddle. Mounting was painful but not impossible. He settled down, considered staying to shoot it out once and for all, then rode southward again.

He knew where they headed. Beth Randall wasn't going to abandon her cargo, and if they hadn't discovered her husband's body locked in the ice, they weren't likely to before reaching Tombstone. The longer they kept the ice covered and out of the sun, the more of it remained to be sold. They had no cause to examine any of the blocks en route.

Dinkins headed south, past Albuquerque and even farther southward, making his way through mountains to get to Silver City. There he'd get the body. He knew unscrupulous men there willing to do anything for a few dollars.

He grinned. That meant they were likely to buy any tall tale he spun about what the wagon's cargo was, just as the others had.

22

"You done got yourself a fever," the doctor said. He scratched his stubbled chin and shook his head. After thinking on the matter a bit, he took off his eyeglasses and began cleaning them using a handkerchief that was gray with grime. "That's what you get swapping lead with someone who's a better shot."

"How'd you know I lost the fight?" Dandy Dan Dinkins sat up and moaned. The doctor has stitched up the bullet wound in his hip but fever wore him down.

"I don't," the doctor allowed. "But you've got the look of a man on the run. That tells me you're running *from* something rather than *to* it."

"Are you a better doctor than a fortune teller?" Dinkins gingerly pulled down his shirt and tucked the tail into his waistband. When it was settled, he fastened his vest and worked his way painfully into his coat. The bullet he'd taken hadn't lodged in his hip but the deep crease had proven worse than an outright hole in his gut. After several days on the trail after the gunfight, the wound had begun to burn.

The day after it burned like fire, he turned woozy and

rotting skin had appeared around the bullet track through his flesh. Only luck had seen him arrive in Silver City before he passed out and died.

"You need a new tailor," the doctor said. He stepped back and held out his hand when he saw Dinkins' stormy expression. "I didn't mean nuthin' by that. I'm a garrulous old coot. Sometimes I don't know when to keep my mouth shut."

If there wouldn't be a hue and cry put up if the sawbones was found dead, Dinkins would have found the right way to keep that yapping mouth shut for good. The doctor was wise enough to see death dancing in Dinkins' cold, flat eyes.

"No charge." The doctor rubbed his hands on his sides. "You fixin' to stay around Silver City long? There's a good boardinghouse across the street." When Dinkins remained silent, the doctor rattled on. "It's run by my sister-in-law. She's something of a gossip but—"

Dinkins made sure his Colt rode easy at his hip, thrust his second six-gun into his waistband, settled his hat squarely and pinched the brim on his way out. A sneer accompanied the polite gesture. Paying the doctor wasn't in the cards, even if the offer for free treatment hadn't been advanced. He considered going down the street to the nearest saloon for a drink, then realized how lightheaded he still was. A shot or two of whiskey would put him out cold under a table.

"We spotted the wagon."

Dinkins spun, hand going to his six-shooter. Antrim lounged in the shade, chewing on the inch-long stub of a quirly. He spat, looked at it, then tossed it away.

"I don't have a match," he said.

"Children shouldn't smoke," Dinkins said. He looked around to see if anyone watched. Being seen talking to the young hoodlum complicated matters when they failed to find any money in the wagon.

Antrim said something under his breath, then pulled back

his coat. An old black powder Remington stuffed into his waistband almost caused his trousers to slide off his slender hips.

"I'm no kid. I'm a man and I know how to use this."

"Where's the freighter?" Dinkins stepped closer and tried to fade into shadow. There wasn't quite enough to hide him.

"A couple miles north of town. They're making good time. The driver might only have one eye but he knows his job."

"Are the others as I said? Two women and a man?"

"Easy robbery ahead," Antrim said.

"Then get to it," Dinkins snapped.

"You're looking old, mister. And frail." Antrim shoved him. Caught off guard, Dinkins stepped back, off balance. The back of his knee hit a chair and he sat heavily. It took all his strength to grab at a windowsill and stay in the chair.

Antrim laughed.

If he hadn't needed the boy, he would have cut him down on the spot. No one treated him like that.

"You move a muscle and I'll chop you down like a rotted tree."

Both Dinkins and Antrim jerked around to see a man sporting a badge on his coat approaching. He trained a shotgun on the youngster. If Dinkins had been stronger, he would have jumped to his feet and shot the lawman.

"Now, Marshal, there's no call for you to point that scattergun at me. I'm not doing anything illegal. Not this time." The boy glanced at Dinkins, daring him to contradict him.

Dinkins wasn't about to provoke the marshal. His plans were more important than salving his wounded pride.

"I saw you push this gent," the marshal said, "but that's not what I want to talk to you about, Billy boy. Miz Newton says you stole clothes off her wash line."

From the way Antrim glanced down at his shirt, there

wasn't any doubt where the stolen clothing had ended up.

"There's some mistake, Marshal," Dinkins said. He struggled to his feet. "If there's a problem with the way he's dressed, well, I'll see to making it right with the washerwoman."

"Mind your own business, mister. This kid's a one-man crime factory. It's not the first time he's swiped clothes from someone's washing." He reached over and plucked Antrim's pistol from his belt. "You and me got some jawboning to do, Bill."

"But—" Dinkins clamped his mouth shut when he saw the determination carved into the marshal's craggy face. He stepped away and watched the law dog march Antrim off in the direction of the town jailhouse.

He almost called out to ask the name of Antrim's partner but held his tongue. Having as little to do with the boy now was the smartest road to travel. He passed a saloon again. His mouth was like cotton and his hands shook from loss of blood, but he pressed on to the livery stable, got his horse and left town. The road into Silver City was hard-packed and easy to travel. The ice wagon couldn't be too far beyond the town limits.

Everything he'd intended Antrim to do he had to do now himself. His injury made that doubly hard, but it didn't matter to him if he killed Randall's widow and her helpers or if some snot-nosed kid it. Doing the dirty deed himself might prove easier in the long run since killing the ice freighters would be easier than gunning down Antrim. That boy had the look of a real criminal. He wouldn't kill easy-like.

Dinkins crested a rise in the road and saw the tall, swaying canvas-topped wagon moving briskly toward him. Dinkins scouted the landscape and made a quick decision. The two women rode horses, leaving the one-eyed muleskinner alone in the driver's box. The other man was nowhere to be seen.

"Scouting," Dinkins decided. "Or riding a ways back to be sure no one tries to overtake them."

The opportunity was limited. He had to do everything just right. Everything. With a curse that turned the air blue, involving the town marshal, Antrim and fate in general, he pulled up his bandana to hide his face. For a moment he sat on his horse, gasping through the dusty cloth. Dinkins pulled it down. Hiding his identity was ridiculous. His clothes betrayed him.

More than that, he didn't intend to leave any witnesses.

A frontal assault was his best bet. If he separated the women from the wagon, he had a chance to commandeer the wagon.

All he needed to do was find the right block of ice and dump it.

Even as he galloped down the steep hill, he realized how foolish that plan was. He needed to recuperate before tangling with everyone in this wagon company. Then it was too late. The driver spotted him and lashed his team with a long blackwhip, veering off the road down a hill toward what looked like a canyon meandering westward into the high mountains.

Dinkins began firing methodically. His aim was off. Hitting anything from the back of a galloping horse was a matter of luck. But his lead blazed close enough to the two women that it spooked their horses. Randall's wife lost control. Her horse ran off, stampeding away from the road.

The redheaded woman cast a quick look at the wagon, then went to rescue her friend who wasn't much of a horsewoman. This gave Dinkins the chance to ride after the wagon.

His horse half slid downhill. He overtook the heavy wagon within minutes. All he had to do was keep an eye peeled for the other man, the one who was all duded up and out of place on the trail.

Dinkins laughed at that. He wore his best outfit because that was all he had left. Bit by bit he had torn the duds he'd worn during the bank robbery and replaced the shirt and pants with his spare clothing. Even then he was filthy from trail dust.

He rode to the wagon from behind to keep the driver from taking a shot at him. The team of straining, braying mules already flagged. It'd come to a halt before long. Until then Dinkins rode closer and peered over the tailgate into the wagon bed. His heart sank. He'd hoped to open the gate and have a few blocks slide free.

They had nailed the gate shut and covered the coffin-shaped crates with a heavy tarp for added insulation. Even if the ice block containing Randall and the map rode at the rear, he had no way to pull it out.

The wagon slowed even more. The lathered team gasped for breath and finally hit a steep incline that stopped them completely. The two lead mules balked and dug in their hooves.

Gun out, he rode around the side of the wagon. He expected the muleskinner to have a gun leveled and ready to shoot. Dinkins wasn't disappointed. The squinting man peered down the barrel of a sawed-off shotgun he'd carried in the driver's box.

"Don't shoot," Dinkins called out. "We can both come out of this as rich men if you listen."

"Whatya sayin'?"

That the double barrels wavered a mite and a torrent of buckshot didn't hurl out in his direction emboldened Dinkins. He hadn't thought this through at all, but the flash of greed on the man's contorted face laid out what Dinkins needed to say as surely as if he read it from a book.

"I'm putting away my gun. You do the same and let's talk." Dinkins looked back up the hill toward the road. Neither the women nor their male companion showed. Yet.

Squinty Houseman lowered his shotgun, then secured the reins around the wagon brake handle.

"You got somethin' to say. So spit it out."

"They're not paying you enough," Dinkins started. This time there wasn't any mistaking the greed on the man's face. He lit up like a prairie sunrise.

"With Mr. Randall gone, the icehouse ain't gonna last another season."

"You'll be out of a job," Dinkins said.

Squinty nodded knowingly. "More 'n that, I heard tell of a company movin' ammonia tanks into Tombstone to make their own ice. It's expensive to set up but cheaper 'n cartin' it all the way from Taos. And the supply's steady, as much as they want to make. They can make ice for the whole danged town of Tombstone. The best Miz Randall can do is sell to one or two saloons."

"You're going to sell the ice in Tombstone?" Dinkins' mind turned over all the possibilities. "Any particular saloon offering to buy it? No, wait, that doesn't matter. What's a good price for the ice?"

"And what's top dollar?" Squinty scratched his stubbled chin. "How much of a cut are you askin' for?"

"I want a block or two for my own use once you get to Tombstone. You can sell the rest and keep the money."

"There's no way they'll let me drive on by my lonesome."

Dinkins cast a glance over his shoulder. Three riders huddled together at the top of the hill, along the road. The man trailing the wagon had shown up. From what he'd seen, Randall's wife wasn't a threat. The other two were. He rushed through his agreement.

"I'll grease the way for you in Tombstone so you can sell

for the best money."

"You can do that?" Squinty turned his good eye around to look harder at Dinkins.

"More money 'n you ever thought you'd see from this job with Pete Randall."

"You know Mr. Randall? We don't know what happened to him. The sheriff said he stuck up the bank and—"

"He won't claim a penny. I'll take care of him. And them." Dinkins jerked his thumb over his shoulder to indicate the trio now beginning the long, treacherous descent. "All you have to do is drive the wagon to Tombstone."

"Mr. Randall? And all three of them?" Squinty licked his lips. "That'll be a shame. That redhead hellion's real purty, but she's as dangerous as a stepped on diamondback. And I ain't got no quarrel with Miz Randall."

"I'll see that your boss' wife isn't harmed. But I guarantee she won't be around to stop you from keeping the money." Dinkins reared back and looked up at the top of the wagon. A breeze blowing from the canyon mouth caused the canvas to snap like a cavalry banner. "Don't forget to get good money for the wagon, too."

"And all you want's a couple of them ice crates?"

"My choice, once you get to Tombstone."

Squinty pursed his lips, sucked on his teeth, then thrust out his grimy, callused hand. Dinkins hesitated, then shook on the deal. This had gone better than he had any hope for when he left Silver City.

"See you in Tombstone. And don't worry about the three of them." Dinkins put his head down and galloped ahead, disappearing around the bend in the canyon just as Beth Randall and the other two reached the wagon.

His hip hurt like hellfire, and he wobbled in the saddle. But his spirits were higher now than they'd been since he set out after the wagon with Randall's body—and the map.

23

"He surely is smiling a lot," Frank Landry said, staring at Squinty Houseman. The muleskinner broke out in an off-key "Oh, Susanna" that caused Frank to drop back behind the wagon.

The sound of the wheels grinding against Arizona desert did little to drown out the song. Barleycorn slowed even more on his own. When a horse objected to a song, it had to be awful.

"Since Silver City, he's been downright giddy," Emily said. Frank looked at her in surprise. It wasn't often she agreed with him. Or if she did, there had to be a caveat. She rode alongside him.

"Why do you think?"

"I swear I saw someone at the mouth of that canyon. The one where Squinty almost drove when he careened off the road north of Silver City. The man rode off before we reached the wagon. I'm thinking it was Dinkins."

"Your eyes are better than mine. I never saw anyone, but you were closer. You and Beth."

"Trouble never just evaporates," Emily said. "If anything,

it condenses and gets worse over time, like that witch's brew you peddle as whiskey." She clucked her tongue in disapproval. Before he responded to her maligning Mudflats Distilling Company's product, she asked, "Why did Dinkins give up trying to steal the ice?"

"Because it's pretty much worthless?" Frank said. "Or maybe he decided it wasn't worth the effort. I winged him. That would be enough for most outlaws to give up and look for an easier target."

"I did see some spoor," she admitted.

"I pointed out the blood trail for you. Even you could follow it. We should have. I hate leaving such business unfinished." More than this, Frank wondered why Dinkins had been so persistent. Following them from Taos required dedication not found in most desperadoes not wracked with the need for vengeance. As far as he could tell, though they had skinned by with their lives several times, killing them hadn't been the primary reason to go after the wagon.

"Getting the ice delivered is more important," Emily said. Again, she surprised him. There wasn't a peep of protest how he had insulted her tracking abilities.

"Squinty hasn't brought up selling the ice on his own, has it? You said he wanted to deliver the cargo by his lonesome."

Emily looked thoughtful, then shook her head. "He hasn't mentioned it again. If anything he rattled off a list of saloons where Pete sold the ice before."

"Helpful, that Joe Houseman," Frank said sarcastically. "Helpful, even if he denied talking to anyone outside Silver City."

"We'll be there in a couple hours," Emily said. She looked around the barren desert. Rolling on the hard-packed ground moved them along faster hour by hour. The steep slopes and rocky potholes they'd encountered from Taos down to the gap in the Continental Divide had slowed them until they reached this stretch that was made for setting speed records.

The weather in the Sonoran Desert was more pleasant than the frigid temperatures in the mountains, too, but this only gave more reason to deliver the ice as soon as possible. Another month and making this trip would have caused most of the ice to melt by the time they reached Tombstone. As it was, the ice buyers could store their purchases in deep mine shafts where the temperature was uniform and insulating sawdust worked even better than in the freight wagon.

Frank Landry looked at the still heavily laden wagon with some pride. He had shepherded it well, fighting off the elements as well as road agents.

"What do you think Beth will do after the ice is sold?" Frank asked.

"I don't know. The High Lonesome Ice Company is pretty much out of business with her husband gone." Emily trained her bright emerald eyes on him. "Do you think Pete was part of the robbery?"

"You're the gambler," he said. "What odds would you give that he wasn't?"

"I'd lose money even at a thousand to one," she said. "But he didn't cut down the bank president or the marshal. Pete's not like that. I didn't know him too well but I trust Beth on that score."

"Defending himself might make him a different fellow." He didn't bother adding that Pete Randall had chosen to take part in the robbery to save his wife the humiliation of their company going bankrupt. That put into question what else he was willing to do.

Frank stood in the stirrups. A dust cloud in the distance betrayed where Tombstone lay. A smelter pumped out heavy black smoke as it produced silver from the mines.

"Why'd Allister not tell me you were also assigned to finding Ochoa's killer?"

Frank laughed. "He knew you'd never keep it a secret. I wanted to work undercover." He didn't bother with the truth that Allister Legende hadn't contacted him and that he'd chosen on his own to help her.

To show her up. Frank looked sideways at the fiery redhead. Maybe there was more to it than his personal pride. She had to admit he had helped and deserved some laurels for it.

She snorted. She knew that was as big a lie as he'd ever told in all his born days. He didn't bother trying to explain his motives. He wasn't sure of them himself.

With a quick tap of his heels on Barleycorn's flanks, he darted forward and rode alongside the wagon. Beth turned to him. Her drawn face showed strain as great as when he'd first seen her back at the icehouse. The trip had drained her energy—and that hadn't been too great to start with, worrying about her husband.

"Squinty says there's an ice broker just outside town that Pete used before. Rather than going from saloon to saloon, he sold the entire cargo there, for a small commission." Beth heaved a deep sigh that turned into a shudder. "I want this over. I'm willing to lose a few dollars in exchange for total sale to one buyer."

Frank nodded in understanding. But this contradicted what Squinty had said earlier about he and Pete knowing the saloon owners and selling individually to them. That lie made him even more interested in a rider galloping along some distance down the road. At first he thought it was a mirage until it darted off at an angle, unlike any heat shimmer induced phantom he'd ever seen. He peered past Beth. Squinty had seen the rider, too.

His smile grew so big it must have hurt the corners of his mouth. Frank instinctively touched the butt of his Colt Navy.

"It ain't far off now," Squinty said. "That way." He pointed off the road in the direction taken by the horseman.

"Tombstone is straight ahead," Frank pointed out.

"The ice broker's yonder. You can take it on in by your lonesome, if you have a mind. Or we can do it the way Miz Randall gets the most money."

Frank wasn't going to argue the point. He set off ahead of the wagon, finding a poorly travelled road that led to an adobe building. If a man hadn't come out and lounged against the wall in the shade, Frank would have declared the place abandoned.

"You got a load to sell?" The man hitched up his drawers and came over when Squinty lashed the reins around the hand brake. "I got the money for you."

"Do tell," Emily said. Frank saw she was as suspicious as he was, but he said nothing. Better to see how this played out before making an objection.

"Check the ice," Squinty said.

"I've done business with the High Lonesome Ice Company before. Where's the owner?"

This set off a round of explanation. Frank took the opportunity to circle the adobe. His first impression this was abandoned seemed to be confirmed by the lack of water in a trough for animals. A buggy with a horse still in harness shifted around in the hot sun, as if the ice agent had just arrived.

He made a complete circuit and returned to the freight wagon to see Beth shake hands with the man.

"All done," she said. "All you need to do is pay me and the ice is yours."

"Let's you and me ride on into town. I got a buggy for

your comfort. A few minutes in the bank will deliver every red cent you're owed."

"What about the ice? Should we drive it on into Tombstone?" Emily hadn't dismounted. She kept her hand near the rifle stock.

"Leave it here," the ice agent said.

"That doesn't seem a good idea. This is a lawless territory," Frank said. "Or so I've been told. We wouldn't want anyone coming by to steal the cargo."

"If that concerns you unduly, let your driver stay here. You and the other lady can, too," the man said. His shifty eyes told of a world of theft and death.

Frank saw the real threat being to Beth Randall. He and Emily spoke at the same instant.

"I'll ride with Mrs. Randall," they both said.

"Good enough. You can go on ahead or ride with us. Your choice," the ice agent said.

"Are you up to staying with the ice by yourself, Squinty?" Emily leaned closer to ask the question, as if the ice agent wouldn't hear the response.

"I surely am. I'm tuckered out from the drive. Let me get into the back and stretch out on top of one of those crates. It'll be cool and nobody'll steal nuthin' whilst I'm on guard."

Frank almost asked how Squinty could catch a nap and still protect the ice. If he wanted to see the end of the trail, he had to let this curious play come to its own conclusion. He silenced Emily and inclined his head toward town.

"We can get a decent bath," he said. "And a feather mattress on a big bed."

"You can go—"

She was cut off by the buggy rattling around the adobe. The driver snapped the reins and sent the horse galloping off, the buggy kicking up huge clouds of dust.

Frank and Emily trotted after the buggy and quickly

reached the road going into Tombstone. Frank drew rein and beckoned to Emily to stop.

"What is it? We can't let that charlatan be alone with Beth. There's no telling what he'll do."

"Leaving Squinty alone with the cargo isn't such a good idea, either," he pointed out. "I don't know what devilment's in store in Tombstone, but she stands to lose the cargo with Squinty watching it."

Emily twisted back and forth, torn between her friend's safety and the ice.

"There's two of us. Keep Beth out of trouble. I'll watch Squinty." Frank touched the butt of his Colt. Unless he was completely wrong, he'd do more than watch.

"Very well," Emily said. She rode closer and reached out to touch his arm. "Be careful."

"That's about the first time you've told me that," he said. He tried to lean out to give her a quick peck on the cheek. She yanked her horse's reins to move too far away for that. Without another word, she galloped after the buggy.

Frank laughed ruefully.

"It's just you and me, Barleycorn. Let's see what trouble we can get into." He had ridden hard from the adobe. He retraced his trail at a more sedate pace. Whatever was going on needed time to develop. It wouldn't do if he disturbed the progress, not if he wanted to find out what was really going on.

Rather than approach by the road where he'd be spotted immediately, he veered away, found an arroyo and rode along the sandy bottom to curl around behind the adobe. He stood in his stirrups to locate the house. A grin spread on his face. He'd been right. A horse was tethered out back that hadn't been there before.

Frank secured Barleycorn's reins to an exposed mesquite

root, then pulled himself up the steep embankment. He stayed low to keep from being seen by anyone in the house.

He went to the side and started to look around when an explosion lifted him off the ground and threw him down so hard he lay stunned.

24

Frank Landry stared at the cloudless blue sky. His eyes refused to focus right away, but when they did, the view wasn't much changed. Blue. Everywhere. In the distance he heard excited voices. And his nostrils flared with the tang of sulfur. A distant, faint voice in his head whispered, "Dynamite."

"They blew up the wagon," he said through shock-thickened lips. Frank tried to sit up and failed. He rolled onto his side, came to hands and knees and finally forced himself erect. His balance returned after a few shaky steps.

Back pressed against the adobe building, he took the time to recover from the explosion. It had scrambled his senses. When he heard two men arguing, he chanced a quick peek around the corner. Gleaming shards of ice lay scattered for several yards. The stick of dynamite had detonated directly under one block of ice, shattering it into crystalline pieces that turned into rainbows caused by the desert sun.

For a moment all he saw was a pair of boots sticking from one end of what remained of the ice. Then he made out shadows and shapes. The rest of a body inside the ice had been exposed when the explosive devastated the ice. A stiff arm thrust outward, as if pointing accusingly at him.

"I've got it," cried a man in shabby clothing that had once been fashionable.

Dinkins!

This was the outlaw he'd shot it out with on several occasions. The man limped as he moved around the ice with the body embedded in it.

A few quick brushes of splintered ice opened a way for the injured outlaw to dive down. He fumbled about, then yanked hard. He held up part of a coat. The paper sticking from it captured Frank's attention. Frozen at first, the dilapidated sheet quickly turned soggy as the ice melted away.

"Gimme," Squinty said. "I wanna see it."

"It's safe with me. I'm not going to let a gust of wind steal it away." The man mimicked releasing the paper and then grabbing for it.

From his vantage point, Frank saw instantly what the road agent intended.

"No! Squinty, look out!" He stepped around the corner, hand going for his six-shooter.

Frank was too late by a heartbeat. Squinty watched the paper flutter about high in the air, held in the man's left hand. The outlaw's right hand moved like lightning to draw and fire. Squinty Houseman gasped, clutched at his chest, then looked down. A look of surprise was replaced by one of abiding anger.

Then he died.

The gunman whirled around, the muzzle swinging toward Frank. The next shot tore away a hunk of adobe wall just over Frank's head. Before another round came his way, Frank was fanning his Colt. Two shots knocked off larger pieces of ice. One bullet probably lodged in the dead man's still-frozen carcass. A third skipped along the surface and ricocheted up into the gunman's belly. Dinkins grunted and doubled over. He dropped to his knees.

This hid him behind the ice, so Frank had to make a snap decision how to approach.

"Give up. You're carrying my lead in your gut. And from the way you limp, I hit you a while back on the trail."

"You're not going to take me in. What are you? A federal marshal?"

"Something like that," Frank said. He had never quite worked out his position in the Society of Buckhorn and Bison. While he had never been sworn in as a lawman, he acted like one when sent out on missions by Allister Legende.

"Then you know what this is." The scrap of paper thrust above the edge of the ice was intended to distract him. Frank didn't fall for such an obvious ploy.

"The Taos bank loot," Frank said. "Your partners double-crossed you and buried it. That's the map." He drew a bead on the spot where he expected the man to pop up. "That's Pete Randall in the ice, isn't it?"

"I shot him but he got away from me. We made off with a pile of money. Him and Wilson buried it 'fore we divvied it up. And that damned sheriff! He wouldn't let us be."

"And you're the only one to survive. Why'd you shoot the bank president? You were on the way out of town. He wasn't armed."

"That was an accident." There was a long pause. "Is him getting ventilated why you're after me?"

"Reckon so, but the money from the bank is a powerful attraction, too."

"There's a reward?" Dinkins asked. "It can't be as much as half the loot. Let's split it, me and you. We ride out in separate directions and nobody's the wiser—and we're both a damned sight richer. I never got a count on the money, but it's got to be ten thousand or better."

"That's more than I'd make in a year," Frank allowed.

"So let's partner up. I have the map. We ride back into the Sangre de Cristos, find the loot and split it. Then we ride our own trails and never see each other again."

"That's a mighty attractive proposition," Frank said. "I'm coming out. Don't shoot." He boldly stepped away from the building.

His adversary rose. A scarlet flower blossomed on Dinkins' belly, but he wasn't any worse for it. His gun hand was steady and his aim good—as Frank had anticipated.

Using his momentum from moving out, Frank threw himself parallel with the ground. He fired as he dived. Dinkins' rounds tore off another hunk of adobe wall. Then the rest of the lead whined past harmlessly. Frank grunted from the hard landing, but he had his pistol trained on the outlaw.

"Drop the gun, you lying snake."

"I thought you were throwing down on me," Dinkins said. "Here. I'm putting it down." He dropped his six-gun on top of the ice.

Frank awkwardly got up—and almost died. Dinkins had a hideout gun that appeared like magic in his hand. One hunk of lead took off Frank's hat. Another made him jerk as it burned across his right arm. The shock of impact caused his entire arm to go numb. He frantically grabbed, picking up his dropped pistol with his left hand.

He fired at the same instant as Dinkins.

The outlaw yelped and dropped his second six-gun. Frank's round tore the length of his forearm. Dinkins grabbed then turned to stone. He stared at the six-shooter Frank clutched in his left hand.

Obvious calculation ran through the man's head. He faced a right-handed gun slick who was forced to fire left handed now. How many rounds had been fired? Was he up to seizing his own dropped pistol and firing left handed himself?

"No." All Frank said was that single word. The fight drained from his opponent like water running out of a punctured rain barrel.

"You got me. I give up."

Frank gripped his gun firmly, making it seem as if he was able to shoot lefty as well as using his right hand. He circled the pile of crushed ice and looked down at Pete Randall's body. One arm had been blown off. The ice had broken away from his body and now melted in the sun.

With a quick grab he snatched the map and held it up the best he could. For being trapped in a dead man's pocket and carted halfway across New Mexico Territory in a block of ice it was in decent shape.

"Think on it," Dinkins said. "We split it, you get new clothes." He looked down at his. "They call me Dandy Dan Dinkins and I am sore in need of another suit after the beating this one's taken the past couple weeks."

"I know you from a poker game in Denver," Frank said. He crammed the map into his pocket and wondered what to do about Randall. There wasn't much he could do, all shot up the way he was. Forcing Dinkins to dig a grave wasn't too likely, either. The man wobbled where he stood.

Frank took some measure of pride in the way he'd shot up the road agent. Hip and belly and now his right arm.

"Let's fetch our horses and see if the Tombstone jail has a spare cell waiting for you."

"Take the map. All the money. Let me go. There's not a reward on my head. You won't gain anything by taking me in."

"Nothing except knowing I've put a killer behind bars."

"Randall shot the Taos marshal. And the banker man. If it wasn't him, it was Hugh Wilson or one of the Chandler brothers. They were kill-crazy. I didn't have anything to do with gunning anyone down."

"I saw how you gunned down Squinty. How many more along the way?" Frank motioned with his pistol. He was beginning to feel like Dinkins looked. The sooner he turned the outlaw over to the town marshal, the better.

25

Frank Landry closed his eyes and drifted off to sleep. The smell of fine tobacco, polished leather and something more, something soothing, kept him from his usual wakefulness.

"A drink, sir?"

He snapped awake and looked up into Kingston's impassive face.

"Bourbon," he said reflexively. It didn't surprise him when the butler turned and showed a silver salver balanced on his fingers, a cut crystal glass filled with two fingers of shimmering amber liquor. Kingston anticipated needs as well as any servant Frank had ever seen. Only the man was more than a servant. His tailored jacket hung open slightly showing the shoulder rig and the pistol nestled under his left arm.

Frank had seen the man in action. Kingston was quick on the draw and deadly with his aim.

He looked around the council room at the rear of the Society of Buckhorn and Bison headquarters. The ride back to Denver had been uneventful. He hadn't hurried, letting his injuries heal as he retraced the path to Taos and then to

Denver. In spite of how long it took, he had beaten Emily O'Connor here.

"I stopped in Santa Fe to finish the poker game I started," came her lilting voice.

Frank never turned. "How much did you win?" he asked over his shoulder.

"Enough," she said. The radiant redhead settled into a leather chair across the council table. "No, not enough. More than enough."

"The governor was never much on calculating odds," came a deeper, more resonant voice. "That's why he's on his way out as governor." Allister Legende strode in. Kingston handed him a goblet filled with red wine. From somewhere he conjured up one brimming with white wine for Emily.

As silently as he served, he backed away and left them alone in the large room.

Frank's eyes drifted to the mantle with its row of bullets, each of a different caliber. Those represented agents of the Society. One of the cartridges had been placed on its side. Another member dead or missing. But his .36 round and Emily's .45 derringer round had been moved to the front edge of the mantle.

"I received a report that our Mr. Dinkins was tried and convicted of killing Joe Houseman. He is sentenced to hang at the Yuma Penitentiary in a few weeks." Legende sipped his wine and made a face. He set the goblet on the end of the table. "Please report. Ladies first." He bowed slightly in Emily's direction.

"The fake agent who drove Beth Randall into town hopped out of the buggy in front of the bank. He walked straight through the lobby and out a side door. By now he could be anywhere."

"Mexico," Legende said. "He is of no consequence. Go on."

"Beth sold what remained of the ice for a tidy sum. She decided not to return to New Mexico and caught a train for San Francisco. I believe she is settling in well there."

"She is. A Society member has checked on her well being. I saw to it that her husband was buried in Tombstone. His part in the bank robbery will not besmirch her reputation, even if we knew exactly what his role was."

"Dinkins said Randall killed Jaime Ochoa and the marshal." Frank worked on the bourbon. It left a warm pool in his belly and relaxed him even more.

"We'll never know. Since all the robbers are, shall we say, no longer with us, and Dinkins will swing for another murder, the matter is settled to our patron's satisfaction. The stolen money has been located and returned to the bank."

"If Ochoa was slated to be the next governor, who takes his place?" Frank was interested in knowing. His deal with moonshiner Buck Isaacson making the Taos Lightning depended on how active enforcement of that blue law was.

"That's none of my concern. I abhor politics, as much as I am up to my ears in such dealings," Legende said. He made a move to take another sip of the wine and held back. "Your illicit manufacture of moonshine can proceed—for the time being."

Frank sat a little straighter. He had never mentioned this to Legende. Keeping secrets in the Society proved more difficult than he liked.

"I had intended to wire you to provide Miss O'Connor help, but you did that on your own."

"I, uh, anticipated your desire in the matter," Frank lied.

"I am sure you did," Legende said dryly. He glanced toward Emily, who sat contentedly sipping her white wine.

"Are there any loose ends that need to be tied up?" Frank asked.

"All is well," Legende answered. He turned and rolled the

single cartridge laying on its side about. "All but for one thing."

"Another assignment?" Emily asked. She looked at Frank.

He wasn't sure how he felt about teaming up with his ex-wife again. He had muscled in on her assignment. In spite of arranging how to set up a lucrative moonshining operation, all he had gotten out of it were bullet holes and ruined clothing.

Allister Legende picked up the bullet and held it between thumb and forefinger. He looked grim as he held it out.

"Don't stray too far. I'll let you know. Soon."

Frank Landry downed the rest of his fine bourbon. He looked from the bullet representing another Society member held between Legende's fingers across the table to where Emily shifted nervously, anxiously in her chair. She was like a racehorse in the starting gate, eager for action. If and when Allister Legende decided who to send on the seek-and-find mission, Frank Landry would be ready. With or without Emily O'Connor at his side.

Until then he had a moonshine operation to start. If he wanted to play with real lightning, there was always Jenny Babson to add some danger and spice.

The End
Gunsmoke and Ice

ABOUT THE AUTHOR

Brody Weatherford is a crusty old rapscallion with dozens of blood-churning Western pulps to his credit published under a host of trail-blazing pen names. He lives somewhere west of the 100th meridian in a spacious log home with three dogs, ten cats, and a palomino named McGee.

COLD FIRE!

"Do you know anything about this man?" Harry asked.

Chico thought for a moment. "I know that he is an evil man. Nine days ago, he took a knife to a prostitute in Miami. She was just a girl, trying to make her way." He shook his head. "Kendrick had no reason to do that."

The cold fire inside Harry's belly froze over a little more. He'd seen Ellen Lafferty's face up in Charleston a month ago. Her father had brought her to the meeting with Harry.

"Kendrick doesn't need a reason to cut up women," Harry said. "He just enjoys doing it."

Chico nodded. "Are you here to kill this man?"

Harry nodded. "I am."

"Then I will wish you good fortune, and here we will separate ways because I do not wish to be part of this. I will fight for my life, but I cannot kill a man in cold blood."

Harry nodded and didn't point out that the old man had to have suspected what was going to happen. He put his heels to his Morgan and rode toward the hut.

"I will say a prayer for you," Chico called back.

COLD FIRE!

"I never turned down the good Lord's help," Harry said.

He dropped his hand to the butt of the .50-caliber Tranter double-action revolver holstered at his right hip.

> Get The Guns of Legende #4:
> Queen of the Bandits

LOOKING FOR OTHER WESTERNS TO KEEP YOU UP AT NIGHT AROUND THE CAMPFIRE?

Try The Punished, a dark western trilogy from
Western Fictioneer Lifetime Achievement Award winner:
Jackson Lowry

Undead
Navajo Witches
Bayou Voodo

Made in United States
North Haven, CT
22 September 2025